Try Again

RICHARD BETZ

PAGE PUBLISHING, INC.
Conneaut Lake, PA

First originally published by Page Publishing 2021

ISBN 978-1-6624-3044-2 (pbk)
ISBN 978-1-6624-3045-9 (digital)

Printed in the United States of America

Introduction

FOLLOW THE DUNCAN family as they grow and adjust to the problems they face in and around the fictional town of Deergrove. Born with an inherited abnormality, the main protagonist, Robby Duncan, skillfully handles the assaults directed at him. His sister, Gina, is not so lucky as she creates an "invisible world" into which she escapes to hide from the cruelty around her.

Parental guidance grounded in understanding and openness is used to address bullying of the Duncan children as they move through middle school years and on to high school. Negative peer pressure spreads among many children as they strive to fit in and maintain friendships, and the children of Deergrove School are no exception as they taunt and ridicule others who are meek and defenseless.

The necessity of the forgiveness of others as well as self-forgiveness are demonstrated throughout childhood growth experiences as youngsters learn to see their shortcomings, dust themselves off, and try again. In addition to addressing the cancerous problem of bullying, learn about recessive gene inheritance and the workings of the human heart as it fights off bacterial invasion.

1

HE WOKE UP in his hospital room and looked through myopic eyes at the whiter-than-white surroundings. Although unable to focus without glasses, revelation of what he had just gone through was like scales falling from his eyes. Robby Duncan tried to focus as his mother cooed lovingly at his bedside, spraying feelings of concern and love on him. Since his birth thirteen years earlier, Liz Duncan has been caught in a quagmire of guilt because of her son's congenital problem, alternately blaming herself and her husband as well as long-dead relatives.

Gina, Robby's twelve-year-old sister, bounded into his hospital room after school and was much relieved to find her brother awake. She had been having nightmares for the past few nights as her subconscious wrestled with the fact that her brother was finally going to get "his problem" fixed. The Duncan family never talked about Robby's condition directly; referring to it as his problem was the way they verbally dealt with his deformity. When a situation persisted for long periods of time, looking at it as having a solution somehow made it seem more tolerable and even manageable, and this was how Gina learned to deal with all concerns. Like the pre-algebra problems at school, she came to the realization that there was always a solution; therefore, Robby's problem would be solved in time by moving the x's to one side of the equation and the numerical values to the other. However, troubles with multiplication and division surfaced in Robby's case.

There was a dull throbbing in Robby's heavily bandaged right hand. The operation to separate his middle finger from his ring finger was not without incident. The team of surgeons wrestled with the question of how to best make the zigzag incisions for bone separation and how much skin grafting would be necessary to have the best result. Although detailed X-rays and an MRI clearly showed complex syndactyly, the operation was not without risk.

Syndactyly—a word that comes from the Greek *syn* "together" plus *daktulos* "finger"—and is a rare genetic condition that occurs in either a simple or complex form. Robby's condition was complex, meaning the bones of the adjacent digits are fused. In simple syndactyly, fingers are joined by soft tissue only.

Mrs. Duncan fumbled in her purse for Robby's glasses. With these in place and an ability to focus, he looked like the geek he never wanted to be! Since he was ten years old and began playing organized basketball, he wore contacts, and his recent migration from troublesome lenses to the Acuvue product was a great improvement. He told himself he could see much better than he could with glasses. In reality, his self-image, although well developed by the sixth grade, showed the greatest improvement.

For the past few hours, house doctors and the surgical team scurried in and out of the hospital room. Although the primary surgeon, Dr. Gottlieb, was confident that the operation went well and that the recovery time of three to six months would evidence fine results, staff members were filled with reservoirs of doubt about the prognosis. Dr. Gottlieb's specialty was vascular surgery, but he had never treated anyone with complex syndactyly. A few years earlier, very successful results were achieved for a patient with simple syndactyly; fingers that were joined by soft tissue were surgically separated. Cutting and separating bone for Robby was a much more difficult and daunting task that called for expertise in sharing bone structure for the two digits by alternately sawing bone at forty-five-degree angles, separation of the webbed fingers, and grafting of skin from the upper thigh.

After Robby awoke, his every-four-hour routine of having his blood pressure and temperature taken began. An intravenous needle secured to the top of his left hand fed medication into his bloodstream. At 4:00 p.m., Robby felt curtains of fever envelop his whole body. His temperature soared to 104 degrees, and he froze in supine position, percolating with fever; with colorless countenance, he looked flat and motionless as newly laid carpet on a living-room floor. Mrs. Duncan rang for a nurse, and Robby's room rioted with help. Gasping for air, he was hooked to respirator and quickly wheeled from the room.

2

THE DUNCAN FAMILY moved to an apartment they purchased on the south shore of Long Island in 1991 during an economic downturn in the economy that saw family resources dwindling both in their family and families around them. Each day seemed to dawn a new revelation; like the sunrise, it never stopped coming. Firstly, the family business of in-ground swimming pool installation started losing money for the first time since 1962 when Thomas and Eva Duncan started the business. Years later, Eva had a stroke that severely limited her abilities to keep the books for the company. The left side of her body was affected, and she had a difficult time negotiating steps in their three-story Long Island, New York, home. The left side of her face drooped, and this once-perky woman with eloquent speech and body movement could not enunciate well. Although her resolve to continue as she had before the stroke was sheathed in granite, her slurred speech and physical deformity belied her efforts and was a constant embarrassment to both her and her husband at the local country club. She was only forty-five years old! Thomas continued to play golf, his first love, and evening meals now consisted of take-out Chinese and Italian food. Like the early morning fog on a clear summer day, enjoyable dinners with friends at the country club were distant memories. As Thomas started to slide into the doldrums of despair, this once-confident and generous man seemed to have little to give. When there is little left, it is time to give expectations, so Thomas declared that a clean wound healed best, and it was now time to close the business and permanently move to a more-manageable apartment living in Sandy Beach, Long Island, an incorporated village on the Atlantic Ocean.

Thomas Duncan Jr. was attending Miami University and was the captain of the golf team. He received the decision of the family move via voice mail in his apartment after returning from a date with Liz Saunders. Liz, from Cherry Hill, New Jersey, and he had been dating since his sophomore year, and it was understood that they would get married after they both graduated in 1991. For the past four summers, Tommy worked with his father in the family business, and his insipid manner when it came to pool sales did little to stem the tide of the failing business. While the information about the pool business fountained out of his father, Tommy inherited his father's love of golf and little else.

After the 1993 wedding at Ricardo's, a swanky and popular reception spot in Cherry Hill, Tommy and Liz moved to Deergrove, Long Island, to be near but not too near his father and ailing mother. Why this town was called Deergrove was a constant topic of conversation among locals as well as visitors to the town. There hadn't been a deer sighting in the town in as long as anyone could remember, and any grove had long ago been cleared for housing.

Over the years, Tommy's mother began to slide deeper and deeper into an ever-bubbling cauldron of self-pity; her unsteady walking was like marching with swaying gait of a windup doll. She gained weight, and her husband sadly thought of her as a popular toy, a Weeble, that was advertised with "Weebles wobble, but they don't fall down." Her deformed mouth always seemed to be a slightly open, redolent of a young bird expecting food.

After a two-week honeymoon in Hawaii, Tommy and Liz Duncan settled into their three-bedroom Tudor-style home on Maple Street in the town of Deergrove, twenty-five minutes away from where Tommy's parents lived.

Although the rooms were small, they were sold on its castle-like style with steeply pitched roof, overlapping gables, and heavily timbered exterior. After being shown various styles of homes, Liz fell in love with the medieval allure of the Tudor, nestled on a tree-lined street amid split level, cape cod, and ranch homes. The patterned brick framework of their home along with the design diversity of the neighborhood greatly added to residential milieu. Interest in the process of finding the perfect home prompted Liz to get a residential real estate license and begin her career of showing homes in Deergrove, Ocean Pines, and Sandy Beach, Long Island.

Liz had genuine concern for the deteriorating health of her mother-in-law. She routinely picked Eva up on her way home from work. As a real estate sales agent, Liz always seemed to make time to be with her, even sacrificing sales to sit for many hours in their screened-in porch or cozy living room while attending to Eva's every need. Tommy, who worked as a policeman in the Deergrove Police Department, never had time for his mother and would even make excuses to not be around while Liz was keeping her company. He would work the day shift and meet his father or friends at the South Shore County Club to play nine holes of golf or simply sit and talk before having dinner. His father also loved his away time at the county club and purchased a lifetime membership for himself and his son. Thomas Duncan Sr. was a well-respected retired member of the community who sat on the board of the Sandy Beach Civic Planning Association. His prior sales experience helped him mediate disputes between the town and local businesses as well as with residents to ensure that all home improvement was done to code in the stable and conservative community.

During the summer of 1995, Liz found out she was pregnant. She bubbled over with happiness as she left the doctor's office, stopping at her in-laws' house to give them the good news. At first the revelation was like a new lease on life for Eva; nevertheless, her lucid mood was short-lived, as fear for the future quickly took up its usual residence in her deteriorating body. Thomas persuaded Liz to accompany him to the country club to give his son, Tommy, the good news. As they drove into the entrance with the gaudy "Welcome to SSCC" sign—this announcement of South Shore County Club had recently been vandalized by graffiti and boasted a new coat of green and white paint—Thomas Senior was concerned that his daughter-in-law was becoming less talkative. He tried to hide his uneasiness, saying that when Eva was pregnant with their only child, Tommy, she was as silent as a predator in the early morning. Liz knew this was probably not true because prior to her stroke, her mother-in-law was the most social person she had ever met and so very unlike the shell of herself she became after the embolism assaulted her mind and body.

Unable to locate her husband at the country club, Liz asked Thomas to take her back to his house so she could retrieve her car and arrive home before her husband to give him the news. Tommy arrived after 10:00 p.m. and let Liz know he was playing cards with a few of his cop friends over at Jack Simpson's house. Jack was also a cop in the Deergrove police force and Tommy's best friend, and he and Liz had gone to fundraising events, birthday parties, and holiday gatherings with Jack and his wife, Sharon. The comradeship among the police officers in the village of Deergrove was the stuff from which legends were made. None of the officers were corrupt, but they would do anything to uphold the reputation of a fellow officer on the police force.

Tommy claimed that he tried to call to let Liz know he would be late because he was out with the boys. Liz missed the call since she was at her in-laws' home. Their answering machine at home was not working. Tommy had said he would purchase a new one a couple times over the past few weeks. Liz went to the refrigerator and scribbled a note to pick up a new machine at the local Radio Shack the next day. She was very methodical, and her whiteboard "to do" list sat side by side with her grocery needs. Milk, bananas, and yogurt took up permanent residence on this market checklist. She did her best to hide the fact that she didn't believe his account of the evening. Over the many years they had been together, Liz learned to accept the fact that Tommy viewed his devotional duties through clouded water. For the time being, she held the secret of the new life within her, secured in the lockbox of her mind.

After awakening the next morning, Liz went off to work because she had four houses to show to a new client. Tommy was already out of the house and on his way to the 6:30 a.m. briefing at the station before his 7:00 a.m. shift began. Deergrove had a small police force, and officers rode alone in a squad car as they police the community. Tommy liked it this way because usually days passed without incident, and he could rest alone at work so he could have energy for his daily recreational time with his father or cronies before heading home. Most of the time Tommy shed his feckless nature when he took off his uniform. He was very affectionate when at home, but recently domestic life seemed to be less and less important to him. However, life-changing events are life's glue that fasten together hopes and dreams for the future, and Liz believed the cloud of indifference that hung over her husband would be whisked away with the binding knowledge of the birth of their future child.

Liz stopped at Radio Shack and picked up a new telephone answering machine; she would wait for Tommy to get home and record the message. No respectable cop would ever let a woman's voice, much less his wife's, announce that "they were unable to come to the phone and to please leave a message, and we'll get back to you." Shortly after arriving home, the doorbell heralded in flowers and a bottle of champagne that her in-laws sent to congratulate them on her pregnancy.

Although Liz and their families were anxious for them to start their own family, her husband wanted to wait a few more years. Liz brought up the subject on numerous occasions, and Tommy was resolute in the fact that they should wait. Over the two years they have been married, Liz, only twenty-four years old, felt their relationship waning so much she believed the birth of a child would bring them closer together. Each time Liz broached the idea of beginning a family, Tommy became more stubborn and hesitant. His argument and excuses became increasingly illogical and awkward, much like a man walking with shoelaces tied together.

When Tommy arrived home after stopping at the club to have a drink with his friends, he noticed the new answering machine and the flowers that greeted him on the dining-room table. The table was set with a newly ironed tablecloth used only for special occasions, accompanied by candles and wineglasses. A bottle of champagne rested in a bucket of ice. Calling to Liz, who was in the master bathroom, Tommy tried to figure out what might be going on. He entered the guest bedroom, placed his service revolver in its usual resting place in the top dresser drawer, and changed out of his police uniform. He was always so very thankful that he had this separate room for his clothing because the bedrooms were small, and closet space was at a premium. The cramped living space was one of the many excuses he used to put off having children.

Liz was in the shower, and Tommy entered their bedroom, speaking loudly enough to be heard over the cascading water.

"Hey, Liz, what's the reason for the celebration?"

Echoing from the shower, Liz replied, "Get ready for dinner, and I'll be down in a few minutes."

Tommy hooked up the answering machine and sat in front of the TV, watching the news as he waited for Liz. He switched back and forth between *Twilight Zone* and the news channel but could not get himself interested in television. The mystery of the reasons for the celebration intruded into his every thought. He felt as if he were trying to catch fish in a whirlpool as he wrestled with the possibilities. It was not their wedding anniversary. The date they first met in their sophomore year at school—a celebration date he always forgot—was believed to be still months away, and birthdays had already come and gone for the year. It must be that Liz received a promotion to office manager at the real estate franchise where she worked. The possible promotion had been a rumor in the office that Liz had been trying to ignore for a number of weeks.

Arriving in the living room in her favorite dress, Liz looked pert and radiant. This was in stark contrast to Tommy's sweatpants, faded University of Miami sweatshirt, and battered old sneakers, along with his petulant posture as he slouched in his favorite La-Z-Boy chair.

"Thanks for remembering to get the machine. It only took a few minutes to connect us to the outside world," he crowed as Liz sprightly entered the room.

"It was on sale. I hope it was easy to program the greeting."

"Sure was. It looks like you had a busy day."

It had never been easy for Tommy to hide his emotions. His once-shrewd mind had long ago lost its ability to mask itself from Liz. Although unspoken, his bewilderment leaked from him like the drip of a faucet that could not be shut off. Under the guise of disinterest, he waited for Liz to speak.

"Are you ready for dinner, Tommy Gun?" Liz used to call him this because although he was not a very good athlete, during high school, he used to gun down running backs from his middle linebacker position on the football team. He still had an old high school friend who also went to Miami University with him that called him Gunner. The two friends relived their past glory on occasion, and Liz picked up on and further nicked the nickname.

"Sure thing, what are we having? It looks like you went to a lot of trouble to get ready for dinner."

"No trouble at all. We are having Chicken Française, twice-baked potatoes, and spinach with garlic and oil."

Chicken Française was Tommy's favorite meal, and Liz prided herself in preparing it well. She pounded out chicken breasts, dipped them in flour and egg, and sautéed them in white wine, lemon, and butter. Adding chicken broth and Italian parsley as well as onion and garlic were touches she incorporated into the traditional recipe because of Tommy's love of spicy food.

She then added, "For dessert, double chocolate cake and espresso."

Tommy sat down, and Liz asked him to open and pour the champagne. Trying to act like this was an every-evening occurrence, Tommy, dumfounded and turning over possibilities for the feast in his mind, was determined that he would let the meal and the reason for it play itself out. After popping the cork, his hand unsteadily darted back and forth as he filled the wineglasses.

Liz planned the evening's surprise, and because of his seemingly detached manner, she was in no rush to let Tommy know they would become parents in twenty-nine more weeks. For her part, the lack of need to hurry was like not hurrying a golden sunrise with the promise of a beautiful day. After placing the meal on the table in serving dishes, she settled down to let the evening unfold. Tommy's "cool guy" facade became more difficult to fake as he guzzled his first glass of champagne and began placing the sumptuous chicken into his mouth. As he did with beer, Tommy swallowed without regard for the bouquet and taste of the fruity liquor. Although he knew it wasn't, the food seemed tasteless as he cascaded deeper into viscosity that slowed his movements and thoughts while eying his wife across the table as if he were watching an old black-and-white eight-millimeter film.

For her part, Liz calmly served the poultry, potatoes, and vegetable as her hands deftly dealt from serving bowls to plate. Tommy continued to eat, but without his usual animation; he sat lifeless, like one of Liz's collectable snow babies that gazed down on them from a shelf on the dining-room wall.

Liz continued, "How do you like the chicken? It was quickly braised in garlic and onion just the way you like it. I hope it isn't too well done."

"It's perfect, and the potatoes are excellent."

The meal progressed restlessly until it was time for dessert. Liz served the chocolate cake with espresso. The espresso drip coffee pot was a present she bought for Tommy the prior Christmas. Whenever he was at the club, he ordered "expresso." Although he had been corrected numerous times and told it was espresso, not "expresso," he could never get the pronunciation correct. It was like the word "water," which he pronounced as warter, adding the R because this was how it was pronounced in Long Island.

Under the cake plate, she slipped a note that read, "Roses are red. Violets are blue. Should we paint the baby's room pink or blue?"

Tommy's eyes grew large and golden, like the brass buttons on his blue police uniform.

3

LIZ HAD FALSE labor two weeks before her due date. Tommy was called in his patrol car, and he quickly picked Liz up at home and whisked her to the hospital. To their disappointment, she was told that she should go home and rest, making sure to see her gynecologist for the next day's appointment. Liz's mother, Mrs. Saunders, arrived the next day. She quickly took charge, checking and adding to a hospital bag for her daughter, which had been waiting at the ready for over a month. It contained all necessities to ensure a smooth transition from home to hospital. South Shore General Hospital had just recently added a baby wing to their facility, which boasted twelve individual rooms and three state-of-the-art birthing suites that were capable of handling any emergency that might arise during the miracle of life. Because Tommy had missed so many classes for which Liz signed them up to get ready for the big day, Liz wanted her mother to be with her both before and during the birth.

When Francie Saunders, Liz's mother, moved into the guest room, Tommy became more and more distant. Although he got along well with Francie, his discomfort by the visit was difficult to veil because he had to surrender his personal dressing room.

Since his realization and acceptance of fatherhood, Tommy diligently prepared for the baby's arrival by carpeting and painting the third bedroom to get ready for the addition to the family. Not knowing the sex of his soon-to-arrive child, he painted the room in soft pastel tones of yellow and green, and Liz stenciled rainbows below the ceiling molding. With Liz airbrushing clouds on the egg-shell-blue ceiling, the room was now ready to be furnished with a crib, dresser, and changing table. The bassinet where she took up residence during the first few months of her life was newly splashed with green and yellow satin and lace material. It occupied the corner of the master bedroom adjacent to the bed.

Liz had had an ultrasound performed in her doctor's office four months after she found out she was pregnant, and she had the nurse write down the sex of the child and seal it in an envelope. She was determined not to know the sex and keep the secret from everyone; nonetheless, after her false labor, she succumbed to her curiosity and peeked. Not wishing to reveal her weakness—friends and family members knew about the secretive revelation, which was hidden in the family Bible—she did not share this information with anyone. Tommy, her parents, and in-laws were all kept in the dark. Knowing she was carrying a son added to her joy because she knew that Tommy had high hopes for a son. During recent conversations, he, very much unlike himself, had opened up to Liz with his hopes and expectations for a child. Feeling his own mortality, coupled with disappointment and frustration with many of his own shortcomings, Tommy let it be known that he believed that what he did for himself would wilt and fade with his passing. At best, according to life's cycle and remembering only the best traits of the dead, he would be eulogized for his life's finer yet few distinguishing qualities. In contrast, he felt that the goals and accomplishments of his offspring would be immortal.

Francie drove her daughter to the hospital after her water broke. Alexis Strong, the maternity nurse on duty, called Liz's gynecologist. With her mother at her side, Liz prepared herself to wait as long as necessary for the birth of her son. It was a very hot July afternoon as she settled into her hospital gown and could not get comfortable in the too-cold room, as the air-conditioning continually blew a wall of stiff, cold air.

Alternating between feeling chilled and a rush of rising temperature as the contractions came closer together, the bedsheets perspired as much as Liz did. Shortly after an epidural was administered, Liz delivered a seven-pound, twelve-ounce boy. As quickly as water escaped from a colander, Liz's joy was drained as she was told of her son's deformity.

Robby Duncan was born with syndactyly, an autosomal disorder that is inherited because of the mutation of a gene on a non-sex chromosome. Genes come in pairs, and recessive inheritance meant both genes in a pair must be defective to cause the disease. Because both parents were carriers with one dominant and one recessive gene for the deformity, the chances of the children of Tommy and Liz Duncan inheriting the mutation are one in four; Robby was born with two abnormal genes. Chances are also one in four that Robby could have been born normal (inheriting two normal genes) or could have been born a carrier (a 50 percent chance of inheriting one normal and one abnormal gene, making him a carrier like his parents).

Although Tommy considered himself a tough cop, he could not bring himself to enter the delivery room. Previously, he had fainted at the sight of blood during a film shown in birthing class, and he could envision himself passing out and falling across his wife as she delivered their child. This experience soured any chance of him coaching his wife during the delivery. He sat in the waiting room, scurrying back and forth down the hallway to listen to his wife's moans outside her hospital room. Francie found him pacing and counting the ceiling tiles in the waiting room soon after Robby was born. As he walked through the door, he witnessed Liz rocking his newborn son with tears rolling down her cheeks.

Tommy could sense the tension in the room.

Liz announced, "We have a beautiful baby son."

"Thankfully, it's over. I hope you weren't in too much pain. If I could have been here, I would have sat by your side. At least your mother was here to support and help you through the ordeal."

"She was great. Tommy, I have some bad news I must tell you. Our son was born with two of his fingers attached. Other than that, he is perfect in every way."

"What? What did the doctor say about this?"

"He said the condition occurs only in one in a few thousand births and that it is able to be fixed with an operation. He said we should consult a specialist."

Tommy did his very best not to let the reality of the situation open itself up to his eyes and show his bewilderment to his wife. He tried to think of an appropriate response and could only think to ask why the abnormality could have happened. He would wait and speak privately with the doctor and gather as much information as he could about the problem. Holding his tongue, he looked at his wife, sitting like a radiant beauty and proudly nestling their handsome son to her bosom. Much like discussion of the weather at times of crisis, mundane and casual conversation is a serum that is the antidote for keeping calm.

"What are we going to name him?" asked Tommy.

"Anything other than Thomas Duncan III, although he does look a little like your father."

"He looks more like your mother, Francie. Let's name him Francis and call him Frank."

"Come on, Tommy!"

Francie knocked and entered the room. Because she attended the birth and already knew of the deformity, she thought the relaxed atmosphere seemed as out of place as Tommy when he wore sneakers to a formal dinner at her house.

She questioned, "How are both of you, I mean the three of you doing?"

"Just fine," Liz said. "We were just going over names that we thought may be appropriate."

Liz and Tommy previously decided they would name the child only after he or she was born. They were firm believers you grew into your name, and it was a great determinate of the future. Thomas Jefferson Duncan was ruled out because of too much pressure, as was George Washington Duncan. The wait-and-see approach seemed to be the only way of making such an important decision. They had time!

4

LIZ WAS RELEASED from the hospital two days after the delivery, and Tommy proudly picked her and his son up in his squad car. Both parents settled into the routine of waking up for night feedings every four or five hours. Within a few months, Robby was sleeping throughout the night. The name Robby was chosen after many hours of playful discussion. Working alphabetically from a baby-name book, Arnoldo and Alphonso were quickly ruled out. Finally, after laboring a few days and working to the Rs, the namesake of Tommy's grandfather won out, and Robby's birth certificate read "Robert Saunders Duncan." Weeks turned into months, and thirteen months after Robby was born, Liz completed their family by presenting Tommy with a daughter, Regina Eva Duncan.

Gina, as she was called, was a perfectly normal child and did not inherit her brother's condition. After researching the abnormality of syndactyly, Tommy and Liz had amniotic fluid drawn from Liz during her second trimester of pregnancy. Until the results were received, both parents felt the question of health of their second child was like a hangnail from which they couldn't get relief. Finally, after weeks of waiting, they learned that she did not inherit the recessive gene from either of her parents.

Since the birth of his son, Tommy had assumed a more-relaxed manner. His afterwork engagements were drastically cut back, and

Liz became a part-time real estate agent, showing homes in the late afternoon and early evening when Tommy was home from work.

At birth, Gina weighed only five pounds four ounces, which prompted Tommy to quip about her diminutive size, "Three of her is hardly a bite," and she bit deeply into his heart. He was never at a loss for calling her by his pet names; a few of his favorites were dearling, mooncake, and duck lips. Within two months of her birth, Gina developed the habit of smiling and causing her lips to pout out in a protruding manner. By the time she was six months old, Tommy would playfully tell her to make duck lips, and to everyone's amazement, she would puff her lips out as if she were trying to kiss an invisible person she was unable to reach.

A year after Gina arrived, it was decided that the family would not be complete without a dog. After researching breeds, Tommy and Liz settled on setters. Not sure whether to get an Irish Setter, Gordon Setter, or English Setter, a family outing was planned to attend a combined show that featured all three.

After attending the show, which was won by an orange belton English Setter, the choice was easy. Four weeks later, Shenanigan, who had orange beltons or spots and one orange ear, became the newest family member. The pet was purchased from Serendipity Farms, the breeder's kennel name. Shenanigan of Serendipity Farms—her call name was Nanny—quickly adapted to suburban family life. With free run of the fenced-in yard and a dog door, which allowed her into a rear mudroom, she affectionately settled in with the Duncan family.

As Robby grew, his attached fingers followed the normal growth pattern of his other digits. Liz was very protective of him, and she not only covered his hands in baby mittens so he would not scratch himself as he slept but covered both hands whenever he went outside. He wore tiny mittens, color coordinated with his many baby outfits. Masking his right-hand deformity became an obsession for which her family and friends admonished Robby's mother. Although never verbalized, Liz thought of herself and Tommy as bad parents as she condemned both of them within the recesses of her mind for not knowing about the possibility of bearing a child with a deformity.

On both sides of the family, a great-grandparent had the heritable disease. Because this was never talked about, this knowledge escaped her until after the birth of her son. Both her father-in-law and her mother-in-law carried the recessive gene.

5

IN ADDITION TO great sense of smell, dogs have uncanny abilities to realize and comfort us in our time of need. No wonder they are called man's best friend, and in Robby's case, baby's best friend! Nanny slept next to his bassinet in the master bedroom and would not leave the room while Robby remained nestled in his portable basket. After Robby graduated to his own room, she balled herself up under his crib whenever he was an occupant. Robby's guardian had an aversion to the baby carriage where Robby would reside as he slept or played with a mechanical mobile in a screened-in room at the rear of the house. Weather permitting, this was where Robby spent many of his first formative months. Wherever Robby was being placed in his pram, an antique carriage with oversized wheels that was hooded and shrouded with lace, Nanny would prance around like a newly born colt until she was satisfied Robby had been relocated without incident. Then she would take up her usual protective position, lying down next to the carriage.

Wherever Robby went, Nanny was not far behind. Before he could crawl, she would gently snuggle herself next to him whenever possible, and she would lick his deformed right fingers. It was almost impossible to keep the mitten on his right-hand appendage with Nanny around. It was believed that the first words that Robby uttered were "puppy hand," to differentiate his right deformed hand from his normal left hand. His problem was accepted by Shenanigan.

As Robby grew, the servile bond his dog felt for him intensified. Once he was of age to go to school, Nanny would be as alert as a sprinter in the starting blocks when she heard the bus arriving to drop Robby off after school in front of the house. She could tell the distinctive roar of bus number 22, which delivered Robby from any other vehicle's engine—car, truck, or bus—which approached or passed by their house on Maple Street. Anyone who was present would swear Nanny smiled at the sight of him nearing and then entering the house.

On his first day of kindergarten, Robby entered Deergrove Elementary School without his mittens. During the summer months before his school inauguration, he was weaned from wearing the apparel that masked his problem. Actually, Liz, with a noticeable amount of trauma, let him first go out in the yard barehanded. As the weeks rolled on toward the beginning of the school year, Robby was completely oblivious to and comfortable with having one normal and one puppy hand in plain sight for the entire world to see. Somehow, he instinctively knew that hiding his deformity in a pocket, hanging his right hand at his side, or otherwise trying to draw attention away from his deformity by never gesturing with it only drew more attention, causing eyes to settle on his hand as the focal point of attention.

Blending in perfectly well with the other twenty-six children in his kindergarten class, Robby felt accepted and no different than other children. Prejudice and name-calling are flaws that are not inherited; they are learned from our parents and other adults around us. And it was not until second grade that cruelly was directed at Robby. He was called Web Boy, Four Fingers, Webster, and Flipper Four Eyes because he had to wear glasses. His classmates heaped these and other cruel labels upon him only after older children who rode the bus to school with Robby pelted him with deprecating names.

Cruelty is a bond that runs rampant with many children who are not parented well. Unfortunately for Robby, middle-school children who rode the bus with him showed few exceptions. His second-grade peers parroted the belittling names in school, on the playground, and even in hushed tones during class.

Robby's father, Tommy, was deeply hurt when he learned about the name-calling. He went to the school and spoke with the guidance counselor about the problem.

Although Tommy and Liz were impatient to have Robby's hand undergo an operation, they were encouraged to wait at least until he was a teenager. The reasoning was that multiple operations would be necessary, and the longer they put off the first operation, the better because future operations would be fewer and less necessary. This was because a child's hand continued to grow as the rest of his body developed, and growth after an operation on a tiny hand required multiple future surgeries.

Mr. Duncan wanted to confront his child's torturers, but a cooler and more logical approach that he adapted was to talk with Robby and a child psychologist that was available through the police department's medical plan.

After the initial consultation, total family sessions helped Robby develop deep feelings of sorrow, but not for himself! He never retaliated, either verbally or physically, to his troubled tormentors but developed a genuine sadness for children who called him names because they did not know better or because they themselves were riddled with personal insecurities. A nail-hard strength of character that would serve him well throughout his life germinated within him.

Freddy Sanchez, the star basketball player on the eighth-grade Deergrove School basketball team, befriended Robby before Robby entered the fifth grade. Freddy was very familiar with a different kind of prejudice, racial prejudice, which he rose above by playing basketball. Because of his athletic ability, Freddy was very popular in school and throughout the neighborhood. Although three years older than Robby, the boys became best of friends. Friendship, along with love of family and spouse, is a great responsibility, and Freddy instinctively knew this and took his obligation seriously. Although no retaliatory words were ever spoken in his defense, no one would ever call Robby a name while Freddy was around. Robby spent many happy hours at Freddy's house, playing basketball.

When Freddy was five years old, Mr. Sanchez nailed a backboard to the garage; and because Freddy was an outcast even at this early age, he spent countless hours throwing the ball at the five-foot-high hoop. Self-confidence is obtained through different avenues of personal development, and Freddy's ticket to self-assurance was punched by playing with his round ball in the driveway. By the time Freddy was eight, the goal was raised to the standard ten feet, and he was able to dribble and shoot well with both hands.

Nanny accompanied Robby on his two-block run to Freddy's house on Pine Street after school each day. She plopped herself on the lawn next to the garage to oversee Robby's progress at playing the game. She even seemed to nod in approval as he continued to develop his skills. If it snowed, the boys shoveled the snow so they could play; little could get between their friendship and love of basketball.

Robby was a natural! His deformed right hand did not prevent him from dribbling or shooting the basketball. He became expert when close to the hoop; however, because of his acute nearsightedness, when he was more than eight to ten feet away from the net, his ability to score a goal was severely limited. The garage ran along the side of the house, and to his and Freddy's amazement, Robby became expert at throwing the ball against the side of the house and have it sail through the cylinder. He could dribble equally well no matter which hand guided the ball, and when he was within a few feet of the net, he almost never missed, alternating between right and left-hand shots. Reality of his abilities was evident whether he was jumping toward the goal or fading away so his older and much-taller friend could not block the shot. His problem seemed to give him great resolve, as strength of character grew together with his ability as time passed in his best friend's driveway.

6

ROBBY'S SISTER, GINA, was outgoing and friendly. However, by the time she was six years old and in the first grade, brutal treatment of her older brother that she was forced to witness both on the school bus and at school created an anxiety in her that she did not have the ability with which to cope. At times she would verbally lash out at her brother's assailants. When this did not have the desired result of quashing the constant barrages and even further increased the assaults, she retreated within herself. At times, she even became the brunt of jokes because of her brother's problem.

Billy Phillips, who was in third grade and a year older than Robby, became a ringleader of the name-callers. His constant and merciless spoken assaults had the desired effect of causing Gina to stiffly sit in her seat next to her brother during their daily bus ride to and from school. Although Robby ignored Billy, Gina became more and more sensitive and thin-skinned.

One morning on the way to school, Billy looked at the siblings sitting side by side in the middle of the bus; he glared at her and shouted, "You must be a freak too! Gina, do you have webbed toes?"

Robby sat with a determined nod and whispered to her, "Ignore him, and he will simply go away, and if he gets louder, the bus driver will step in."

Gina leaned toward him replied in an equally low voice, "He just keeps it up. When will he ever stop?"

Unable to control herself, she peed her pants.

"Don't worry, and try not to let him know he is bothering you. We will go to Principal Clark's office and call Mom when we get to school."

Whimpering in a low tone, she replied, "Okay, but I hope no one notices my pants are wet."

Upon entering the school, the children marched into the main office.

Because Principal Alexis Clark was in a meeting, Gina asked to see the nurse, Dr. Gottlieb's wife, who knew the Duncan family well, saying she did not feel well. Noticing Gina's wet pants, she called Mrs. Duncan, who arrived within fifteen minutes to pick up her daughter. Gina could not file this incident deeply enough into the recesses of her mind, and she had nightmares for many months afterward. Brutal treatment by children is contagious, and pain and suffering sprouted in Gina like an unattended garden overcome with weeds. To help her deal with her pain, she would lie in her bed at night and pretend that she was invisible. If no one could see her, no one could hurt her.

As Gina spiraled downward into doldrums of despair that her brother never felt, her apprehension led to social problems. Even her interaction with her parents became guarded and defensive. An outlet to help her self-esteem was suggested during family counseling sessions, and she enrolled in Ms. Tina's Dancing School. Possessing a subtle body, her mind began to undergo a parallel transformation during gymnastics classes. A rising tide lifts all boats, and Ms. Tina was the medicine that caused the waves of promise to crest in Gina. Dancing was the magic potent she needed, and her graceful movements helped her gradually develop as the child she was to become, moving forward toward some future imagined joy.

During the next few years of dancing school, Gina took tap, jazz, and toe lessons. The discipline of learning numbered toe-dancing positions and working at the bar while watching herself in the mirrored wall caused self-confidence and self-image to rise like yeast laced flour in a hot oven. During the yearly dance recitals, attended

by her entire family, she was routinely singled out for individual performances in ballet and gymnastics.

Mr. and Mrs. Duncan regularly stopped after the recitals at
Friendly's Restaurant, the children's favorite place to eat. As they
entered the restaurant on this particular late afternoon in January
after Gina's standing-ovation performance, wind whistled briskly and
skipped papers on the sidewalk in front of the building. The entry
door nearly snapped off its hinges as they made their way inside.

Tommy guided his daughter inside, saying, "Bumble Bee, if it
had been this windy during your performance, you would have been
shot out of your ballet shoes."

"And all that work I did making your costume would have been
blown away too," added Liz.

Tommy approached the receptionist still wearing his police uniform because he just got off work before the recital and said, "May
I have a large booth for me, my wife, son, and Lil Cactus Flower."

The waitress smiled as a wave of embarrassment crested over
Gina, and she moaned, "Dad."

Liz, humorless as a chicken when her husband used one of his
many names for their daughter in public, demanded in a whispered
yet stern voice, "Put a lid on it, Tommy!"

Mr. Duncan complied and did not refer to her except by her
name, Gina, until in the sanctuary of the car on the way home when
he addressed her as Jumping Bean.

After they were seated in a corner booth in the restaurant and
removed their winter coats, placing them on the hooks outside the
booth, Robby nudged his mother and told her that Billy Phillips,
their premier tormentor who continually bullied him and his sister,
was sitting at the booth across from them. Robby thought this com-
ment was necessary because Gina underwent a gloomy change as
she sat down and noticed Billy was present in the eatery. As the family took their places, Gina was smiling and obviously proud because
of her performance; nevertheless, Billy's presence laced into her and
caused her high spirit to unravel. She felt as badly as she did on the
day she had to be picked up at school by her mother after the alter-
cation on the bus.

Billy's parents, Mr. and Mrs. Phillips, were present with one of their other children. Having completed their entrees, they were being served strawberry shortcake and ice cream for dessert. Liz huddled the group together for an impromptu family meeting and warned everyone, including her husband, not to confront the family. Mr. Duncan glared at Billy briefly, and whether it was the icy stare or the fact that he now knew Mr. Duncan was a policeman, Billy felt and looked like a scared cat chased up a tree.

The children enjoyed their usual chicken fingers while Liz had a bacon cheeseburger and Tommy a Rueben Sandwich. Each order came with huge servings of french fries, which Mr. Duncan helped the family polish off like he was popping Cheerios into his mouth. Although his six-feet-four-inch frame was getting a little soft in the middle, and he had to loosen his belt to make room for dessert, he felt great satisfaction in the belief that Billy Phillips might have learned his lesson.

During the meal, the wind let up, and the parking lot was covered with a pristine dusting of snow by the time they left Friendly's.

After they settled in the car, Tommy looked at his daughter and said, "Duck Lips, I am so proud of you and the way you performed today."

Robby felt tremendously proud of Gina too; he could not restrain himself from puffing out his lips, coming out with a series of supportive quacks, causing the entire family to laugh lovingly.

On the way home, the family sang "Old McDonald Had a Farm." Although all the animal noises were bellowed in harmony, the quacks were given extra emphasis. It was believed that *the family that sings together clings together* in good times and bad; therefore, it was commonplace that the four family members would sing silly songs often.

Tiny white flakes whispered down through the darkness and guided their way through the glare of the car's headlamps.

7

IN THE UNITED States there are many traditions: flying the American Flag for national holidays, giving fresh flowers and candy for Valentine's Day, Sunday dinner at the grandparents, and fireworks on the fourth of July and New Year's Eve, to name just a few. The Duncan family tradition was the family meeting to discuss matters that affected them. It was believed that sharing feelings in an open manner without fear of being judged tied the Duncans together and that open, honest discussion was at least equal to the bonds of blood coursing through their bodies.

After church and stopping to pick up a dozen donuts at Dunkin Donuts (the dollar-off coupon in the weekly church bulletin was always used), the family made their way to their home on Maple Street in Deergrove, Long Island. With a wry smile, Mr. Duncan always asked for a dozen *dunkins* for the Duncans.

When a full breakfast, usually consisting of french toast that Robby and Gina called square pancakes, had been consumed and the table cleared of dishes, a Sunday Team Meeting was held to decide what they would do for the day. Almost anything goes as the four family members gathered around the kitchen table and wrote down how they would like to spend the day on four-inch square pieces of paper that were folded in half like slices of bread and tossed into an old, crumpled-up fishing hat. This weathered and much-rained-on and deformed, poor excuse for a head covering sat on a hook in the kitchen and was used only for this purpose. Because of its dilapidated condition, when they had company, Mrs. Duncan stashed it under the kitchen sink.

The only meeting rule was that "going to the movies" might not be entered as the weekly family activity. Movies were out because Mrs. Duncan insisted that there must be room for family discussion and interaction on their Sunday-afternoon escapades. Like a magician pulling a rabbit out of a hat, Mr. Duncan made great ceremony about mixing up the four weekly entries and picking the one that would decide their fate for the day. The children routinely penned "roller-skating," "Chuckie Cheese," "bowling," "fishing," and "trip to the zoo." They then crossed their fingers, praying to wish their wish. During the summer months, "go to the beach," "putt-putt golf," and "picnic at the park" got a lot of play. The parents entered such ideas as "afternoon board games," "visit relatives," and "concert in the park." Concerts were free during the summer months.

It's a warm spring day; therefore, the day's Sunday activity might be an indoor or outdoor affair. Mr. Duncan told the children to close their eyes and give him a drumroll.

Mr. Duncan always chanted, "Double Bubble, Toil and Trouble, Cauldron Bum, and Cauldron Bubble," as he mixed up the papers, choosing one. "And the winner is, wait, I can't read this. Is this your writing, Mom?"

Mrs. Duncan looked at the scrawled letters and countered with, "Not mine. I can't guess who scribbled that!"

It was not unusual for Mr. Duncan to palm an entry and fake as if it were chosen from the hat. Today he held up the winner and proclaimed, "Take a nap and smoke a cigar on the back porch."

The children were familiar with their dad's wild spur-of-the-moment substitutions. In the past, he had proclaimed, "Wash the cars" and prior to that "Mow the lawn and weed the garden" and "We're going to the moon" as winners. When he wanted to get to his wife, he had maintained that "Watch Mom clean the house" or "Shop at the supermarket and leave Mom home" to be the chosen activity.

Gina came out with her usual, "Oh Dad!"

"Pollywog, what's the matter? Are we out of cigars?"

For his part, Robby shook his shoulders and gave a deep and phony explosive laugh. This delighted the rest of the family as he mimicked his father's sonorous sounds, which echoed much like a mountain laughing.

"*Et tu Rob Boy*" was clamored in reply. "Back to the serious matter at hand. Where and how to spend the day? Give me another drumroll."

Mr. Duncan again stirred the contents of the hat and leaned over like a circus maestro taking a bow. This time, after rolling up his sleeve and moving quicker than sparks from a fire, he pulled the victorious entry from the hat. "And the outing is…church carnival." Although it was neither of their entries, the children beamed with delight.

A pleasant afternoon and into the early evening was spent going on rides and stuffing faces with cotton candy, french fries, pizza, and funnel cake.

On their way home, the family was in excellent spirits as they usually were when together and enjoying bonding activities. A chorus of the song "N-A-N-N-Y" was joyfully entered into. A popular children's song was "B-I-N-G-O," and this was adapted to the Duncan family pet.

Mr. Duncan led them, "The Duncan family has a dog, and *Nanny* is her name."

Spelling the name, all family members chimed in, "And N-A-N-N-Y, N-A-N-N-Y, N-A-N-N-Y, and *Nanny* is her name."

Mr. Duncan continued his solo, "She is walked, fed, and loved by the Duncan family, and *Nanny* is her name."

Substituting a clap for the first letter, they pounded their palms together and sang, "And clap-A-N-N-Y, clap-A-N-N-Y, clap-A-N-N-Y, and *Nanny* is her name."

Continuing on, the song was complete when five claps were substituted for the letters in Nanny's name. Mr. Duncan delighted the children as he constantly changed his solo parts, and they continued the clapping and spelling refrain, singing the song over and over again. At times he added, "She plays, eats, and sleeps with Robby, and *Nanny* is her name." Spelling, clapping, and squeals of laughter followed such lines as, "Pollywog gets to pick up poop in the yard, and *Nanny* is her name," or "Mrs. Duncan has to vacuum the rugs three times a day, and *Nanny* is her name."

The joyful mood continued for the remainder of the Sunday evening before the exhausted family went to bed early in order to be rested for the upcoming week's school and work activity.

8

MR. DUNCAN ARRIVED at South Shore Hospital just as Robby's hospital bed was being shuttled down the corridor. Stepping aside as he was almost run over by the cocooned child; he did not recognize his son, surrounded by nurses and technicians. When he entered Robby's room, he found: his distraught wife; his daughter, Gina; and the medical surgical nurse on duty, but no Robby! The commotion over the past few minutes left Gina in tears, and Mrs. Duncan was trying to comfort her young child as best she could without any knowledge of what was happening to her son.

Mr. Duncan, with the most recent *Sports Illustrated* in hand, froze as he tried to understand what was happening. His daughter was shaking as if she had just emerged from swimming in the cold Atlantic Ocean on a breezy, cool, early summer afternoon.

"Liz, what's going on? How come Gina is so upset?"

"Robby had 'some kind of reaction,' and he was taken out of the room a few minutes ago."

"Has anyone been able to tell you why? I thought the operation was a success and that he was doing fine."

Judy Roberts, the nurse, who was very experienced because of her twenty-two years of service, was trying to explain what might be happening. Because she had seen so much over her career, she wanted to console the family without giving false hope.

She knew the condition was very serious, and using her professional yet upbeat voice, Nurse Roberts explained, "Robby is in excellent hands. He has been rushed to the post-operative intensive care unit where all his vital signs will be monitored. We have excellent doctors, and I am certain he is receiving the best care possible."

Mr. Duncan, as tense as a guitar string ready to snap, tried to compose himself for the sake of his family, saying, "He has been through so much. I'm sure he can overcome whatever is happening."

Just then, Freddy Sanchez entered the room. He had a get-well card signed by Robby's basketball team with him. As the star of the eighth-grade basketball team—Robby was in the seventh grade when he was moved up to be the starting guard on the team—Robby had earned the respect and admiration of the entire school. The largest signature on the card was that of Billy Phillips, his former torturer, who was the starting center on the basketball team. Above his signature was written, "Hurry back, everyone misses you, your friend and teammate."

Tommy's parents joined the family after they moved to a waiting room to sit and wait for an update on Robby's condition.

Shortly before eight o'clock, Dr. Fischer, an infectious control doctor, entered the room. The family gathered around him as he explained what was going on with Robby.

"Robby is in septic shock. He somehow picked up a blood infection that is being treated with the most powerful antibiotics on the market: vancomycin, gentamicin, and cipro. An additional complication is that the infection seems to have settled in the heart. An echocardiogram shows vegetation or growth on the valves of the heart. Dr. McDade, an excellent heart specialist, will update you as soon as her evaluation is complete."

Robby witnessed the images of the echocardiogram on the computer screen next to his bed through foggy lids that scraped across disbelieving eyes. What he saw caused fear to press upon his soul. Each time his heart pumped, the valves swayed with infection that resembled trees gently blowing back and forth in a steady breeze. Only half conscious, Robby knew something was very wrong as he heard the technician and heart doctor discussing severe heart damage because of damage to the valves. Later a label was given to the germs that resided in his heart—infectious bacterial endocarditis.

The heart is a pump that has four chambers separated by valves that control the flow of blood between the upper two atria and lower two ventricles. Each valve, much like a hot-and-cold-water faucet, is opened and closed to prevent blood from backing up as it makes its way through the heart's chambers and out to into the arteries of the body through the aortic valve. An electrical stimulus generated by the sinus node sends messages that cause the chambers of the heart to contract and pump blood through the valves. The electrical system of the heart controls the heart's rhythm rate and heartbeats, causing the chambers to contract in a synchronized manner. If the heart is beating too quickly (tachycardia) or too slowly (bradycardia), the reason for the arrhythmia or disorder must be investigated. Robby's heart did not fall into either category because the beats were too irregular, sometimes beating too fast, too slow, or skipping a beat.

Only Mr. and Mrs. Duncan were allowed to visit Robby in the infectious control section of the intensive care unit. When they entered the ICU wearing surgical masks, they noticed an additional intravenous line on Robby's right arm. Later they were told this was a PIC line (peripheral intravenous catheter) that was sending the powerful antibiotics directly into the heart to combat the infection. Their anxiety over their son's condition skyrocketed as they learned that there was no certainty that the mitral valve between the left atrium and left ventricle as well as the aortic valve between the left ventricle and the aorta would be able to recover from the infection.

At a meeting with Dr. Sheila McDade, it was explained that although there was an obvious arrhythmia or disorder of the heart rate, an electrocardiogram (EKG) that tested the heart's rhythm rate and heartbeat was unable to pinpoint any abnormality.

Robby's parents were praying that all questions would be answered and he would recover in time to begin high school in a few months. Both Dr. Fischer and Dr. McDade explained that there was no quick and easy way to rid Robby's body of the infections. Many times the practice of medicine was just that; different medicinal drugs did not always react the same in all individuals, so a variety of pharmaceuticals must be tried to see which would have the greatest affect. It was believed that the cocktail of three antibiotics that Robby was receiving would be able to kill the infection that was being pumped throughout his body.

Further investigative techniques to ascertain how much damage was caused would be necessary.

9

DURING GYM CLASS while in sixth grade at Deergrove Elementary School, Robby dazzled the gym teacher, Mr. Robinson, with his basketball skill. He was amazed by the dexterity that was shown at such an early age by Robby, who seemed to be ambidextrous. Whether dribbling with his problem hand or his left hand, he was able to control the ball and easily keep it out of reach of any defender. Additionally, the teacher noticed he could pass and shoot well with either hand. An added benefit was that Robby did not seem to go in for glitzy moves; he would not unnecessarily dribble between his legs just to impress himself and others. He had a well-developed spin move as well as excellent crossover dribble. Robby was a diamond in the rough, and the gym instructor was determined that he would polish up his skills, teaching him the finer facets of the game.

After class, Mr. Robinson approached Robby, asking, "Where did you learn to play so well?"

"From my best friend, Freddy Sanchez. He showed me how to play in his driveway. We practice by playing one-on-one all the time."

In addition to being the middle-school gym teacher, Mr. Robinson was the coach of the eighth-grade boys' basketball team. Last year Freddy had played for him and was the best player on the team. With Freddie as team captain, Deergrove finished in second place in the Southern Long Island Nassau County League. Although Robinson was a good coach and a better example of fine character to his players because of the small size of the school in relation to neighboring towns, his pool of students was limited. Talented players were a rare commodity.

"How would you like to go out for the sixth-grade school team, Robby?"

Coach Robinson did not coach the sixth-grade team; however, he had a lot to say about sports in general and basketball in particular at the school. When he recommended a player for the team, tryouts were a formality; the player was automatically selected to play for the school. In fact, this was how Freddie Sanchez became a member of the squad a few years earlier.

Although Robby was developing a newfound confidence because of his ability on the court, just as he hoped his Sunday team meeting choice would be picked, he secretly hoped that someday he would be chosen to follow in the footsteps of his best friend. He longed to shed the bonds of family protection, harboring a hidden hope for praise from his father, and basketball might cause his star to rise in his father's eyes.

He responded, "Coach Robinson, I'm pretty sure my parents would not go for it. They have always been overly concerned about me and try to constantly shield me from others."

Mr. Robinson was called Coach by everyone at school. He noticed how well Robby shot when he was within a few feet of the basket; however, it was obvious that he would not attempt a shot when he was a distance away. Robby wore thick glasses when not playing basketball, and he continually squinted while not wearing them on the court. His pained expression when he tried to focus caused his forehead to wrinkle. As he dribbled across half court, his furrowed brow made him to take on the countenance of absent-minded professor deep in thought.

The Duncans were very hesitant about letting Robby play organized basketball. With his best friend and in the privacy of the Sanchez driveway, he was not open to scrutiny and the focus of attention along with possible public ridicule because of his problem. Coach Robinson approached Mr. and Mrs. Duncan at *Open School Night* and talked about Robby playing basketball and how it could help bolster his confidence both in school and as a building block for life in high school, college, and beyond.

The coach was bowlegged, so much so that it caused him to look as if he were riding a horse when he walked. Based on his position of authority at school and the respect he earned from students and parents, his labored gait when he walked was completely accepted and considered his trademark by most people. He confided to Robby's parents that his ability on the basketball court cloaked his detractors in social blindness with regard to his obvious difference. After he starred in sports, he never had to listen to comments such as "Where is your horse, cowboy?" and "Why aren't you wearing your ten-gallon hat and six-shooter?"

When he told Robby's parents that the most cutting remarks with which he had to put up were toward his younger sister many years earlier, he struck a nerve. Mr. Robinson's sister was referred to as Trigger, Roy Rogers's famous stallion. At times she had to listen to scowling male classmates who used to chant, "What a face, what a figure, two more legs, and you'd look like Trigger."

Although the players who wanted to play on the sixth-grade basketball team had already been cut, Robby was allowed to try out; and because he was easily the most talented player on the team, he was made captain. The scoreboard and clock flashed information in huge print on each end of the gymnasium. Unable to see the illuminated numbers and not wanting to play while wearing glasses, Robby relied on his teammates to tell him how much time was left in each half of play. This problem was solved halfway through the season when he was fitted for his first pair of contact lenses.

Basketball was not Robby's second chance at life; it was his first! No longer was he called cruel names at school. His greatest detractor, Billy Phillips, also played basketball. A year older, Billy was a member of the sixth-grade team. He did not possess a great deal of talent, but at five feet ten inches tall, he was the tallest player on the team. Billy actually became Robby's defender. If a player on another team mouthed off at Robby because of his deformed right hand, Billy employed dirty tactics to teach the opposition a lesson. A well-placed elbow to the face or groin immediately shut the mouth of the offender. Billy was even thrown out of a game for flagrant fouls while defending Robby on two occasions.

After the incident in Friendly's Restaurant when Mr. Duncan visually confronted him, Billy Phillips felt badly. Nevertheless, from the third through the sixth grade, he kept up his verbal assault because he believed he had an image to uphold. When image takes over the reality of life and growth as child, or for that matter, a person at any age, it is a difficult to shatter the comfortable mold no matter how much it hurts others. This is especially true if it is an image of superiority embedded in feelings of inadequacy. Like roller-skating, after you skate for a couple of hours, it feels funny to walk with your feet firmly planted in your shoes. Billy's skates never seemed to be taken off, and when he did untie them, he was very uncomfortable and ill at ease, balancing on the shaky ground he created. He preferred trying to skate through childhood because he knew no other way, with an unspoken belief that he didn't discover and learn lessons but rather he created them. Feeling he was better than others and lording over those around him kept him from falling.

10

BILLY'S YOUNGER SISTER, Amy, and Gina became friends. This was after Amy joined Ms. Tina's Dancing School a couple years after Gina became the star pupil. The two girls were the same age and in tap and ballet classes together every Saturday morning. Gina did not know that Billy was her brother. This was because Amy never sat with her brother on the bus, and in fact, she was embarrassed by the way he treated Gina and Robby. One Saturday Amy was picked up by Mrs. Phillips, and Gina saw that Billy was in the car.

During dancing class the next weekend, Gina was distant, and Amy knew there was something wrong.

Amy asked, "Gina, don't you feel well? You're not talking to me today."

"I didn't realize that Billy was your brother. We can't be friends anymore because you have such a mean brother."

This cutting off of friendship is common in children when they realize that a sibling or even a more-distant family member has wronged them in any way, and Gina was continuing to have nightmares because of Billy's cruelty.

Amy cried and could not continue with the day's lesson. When her mother arrived at the school, she ran out to the car and let her mother know she was quitting dancing school.

Mrs. Phillips asked, "Why do you want to quit? You were doing so well, and just yesterday you told me how much you love Ms. Tina, the others in your class, and the classes themselves."

"I just quit. I hate it, hate it, hate it."

After they arrived home and Amy refused lunch, Mrs. Phillips went into her room. She was lying on the bed with her head buried in her pillow.

"Tell me what's going on. How can you love to dance one day and hate it the next? You have always been able to tell me anything. Come on, baby, let me know what's bothering you."

Although Amy's mother knew about the mean streak in Billy, like many parents whose children had problems, she was in denial. She believed that the names he called Amy and the way he thought and talked as if he was superior to others was a phase he would out-grow. Billy even had a love-hate relationship with his father. At times he acted as if he respected his dad, and at other times he rebelled. Just asking Billy to take out the garbage could cause him to scowl at Mr. Phillips and even mumble under his breath that he hated his father.

Amy explained why she could no longer continue with dancing school. Her friend, Gina, was continually ridiculed and called names by her brother, and now that the sibling relationship was out in the open, Gina would no longer be her friend. Because friendship is so very important to children, Mrs. Phillips listened to her daughter rant that her life was over!

Upon entering the house after basketball practice, Billy, who was now in the sixth grade, was confronted by both of his parents. Rather than put their daughter through even more trauma by having to confront her brother, Mr. and Mrs. Phillips sat down with Billy to get to the bottom of what was happening during school.

His dad said, "Billy, the most important thing we carry with us is our reputation. I hope you never disgrace our family name. But just as importantly, I hope you don't disgrace yourself because a bad reputation is very difficult to lose after others view you in a bad light."

"Dad, what do you mean?"

"I just found out that you have been calling the Duncan children names and causing problems for them at school and on the school bus."

"No way, Dad. I have never called them names or anything, I swear. Mom, you believe me, don't you?"

"Billy, dear, I don't know what to believe and hope you have not been involved in making those children feel badly."

Mr. Phillips said, "I'm going to call the Duncans and ask them about how you have been treating their children."

Maybe out of guilt, just being caught, or because Mr. Duncan was a cop, Billy began to sob uncontrollably. When caught in a "gotcha moment," the natural instincts of fight or flight took over. With nowhere to run and no way to defend himself, Billy flew into a fit of crying, so much so that he could not even talk. Tears streamed down his cheeks, and his nose leaked mercilessly on to his upper lip. Mom put her arms around him and, handing him a fist full of tissues, told him everything would be all right.

Mr. Philips talked about respect for others and the necessity to treat children the way you wanted to be treated. In a calm manner he spoke of not singling out others because they were different. He explained that picking on others because of their race, religion, or physical handicap was a double-edged sword. It might make you feel good at the time as you put others down, but it would catch up with you in the end because others would never have any respect for you.

Billy could not get control of himself for over half an hour. In the past, his father would spank him to teach him a lesson when he was caught doing something wrong. The few times he was struck did not even hurt and did not teach him any lesson. He kept wishing for the past; a severe beating would be much better than listening to his parents now and feeling the disgrace of his parents knowing his past that now felt like splinters in his heart. The evil stain of guilt was difficult to wash away.

Not able to compose himself, Billy went to his room and chose not to face his family during dinner. Mr. Phillips entered his bedroom and told him it was not the end of the world. There were always chances to make up for past mistakes. He confided that he, too, had made many mistakes that caused hurt to others and himself. Although these wounds might take time to heal, the passing of days and months were great equalizers. He told Billy he would help him devise a plan to help get him out of the corner he was painting himself into.

The next day was Sunday, and Billy came down from his bedroom in a morose mood. His parents and Amy were already sitting at the breakfast table. Reality was his enemy as he hoped the prior evening's discussion would not continue. Mr. and Mrs. Phillips had already agreed that they would give Billy time to think about his past actions. Later in the day, they would present different ideas to him and he would digest the possibilities and they would help him come up with a solution.

His parents called Billy into the dining room at just after four o'clock. He wanted to run, but his legs felt like rubber. Slumping down in his chair, his father demanded that he sit up and listen. Billy would have to choose between continuing his name-calling, ignoring the situation and hoping it would go away, calling on the phone to apologize, or going over to the Duncan house and telling the children how sorry he was for his past actions.

"What should I do? I am scared of Mr. Duncan. Do you know he is a cop?"

"Of course, we know. We see him around town, wearing his uniform, and your mother shops in the same stores as Mrs. Duncan. They are nice people."

"Mom, tell me what to do."

"The choice is yours, but strong medicine shows the best results. If I were you, I would have your father drop you off and wait in the car while you go and apologize to Robby and Gina Duncan."

"All right. But, Dad, will you come into the house with me?"

"Of course, I know you can do this. It is a great lesson to learn. When you hurt with names in person, the apology should be face-to-face."

Mr. Phillips called the Duncan house and spoke into the answering machine, asking Mr. Duncan to return his call.

11

THE DAY'S SUNDAY team meeting resulted in the four Duncan family members and Nanny spending the afternoon fishing from the rock jetties at Lido Beach. Snappers were running, and the five-gallon bucket they took with them was spilling over with these tasty baby-blue fish. Nanny loved to sit and watch the waves, and the family believed she brought luck to them whenever she was able to join them during their family outings. This evening's dinner would fill the family with barbecued snappers, corn on the cob, and baked potatoes.

Just after 5:00 p.m., on the way back from the fishing expedition, Mr. Duncan was in his usual playful mood. There were a few doughnuts in the car that were left over from the morning trip to Dunkin Donuts. Although they were getting a little bit hard, each family member happily consumed one as they made their way back to their home. Even Nanny had her favorite, lemon filled.

Mr. Duncan looked at his wife and crooned, "How about a song, Momma? Why don't you lead us in the Doughnut Song?"

"Pass some napkins to the kids so they don't make a mess."

"Hows 'bout it, Momma?"

Both Robby and Gina cheerfully chimed in, "Hows 'bout it, Momma?"

And with the windows open, all four Duncans harmonized:

Well, I ran around the corner, and I ran around the block,
And I ran right into the doughnut shop.
I picked up a doughnut and rubbed off the grease
And handed the lady a five-cent piece.
Well, she looked at the doughnut, and she looked at me,
And she said, "Why, sir, you can plainly see,
There's a hole in the doughnut, there's a hole right through."
And I said, "There's a hole in the doughnut too."

The playful mood accompanied them into the house as they prepared the evening meal. Dad lit the charcoal grill while mom scrubbed the Idaho potatoes. Once the fire was white-hot, the fish and the corn that was still in the husks were cooked on the grill. Although everyone believed that the potatoes tasted better when baked, in the interest of time, they were wrapped in foil and tossed on the grill.

It was not until almost nine when Mrs. Duncan retrieved the message on the answering machine from Mr. Phillips, and her husband returned the call.

Mr. Phillips was expecting the call, so he answered it on the second ring.

"Hi, this is Tommy Duncan returning Brad's call."

Tommy and Brad know each other socially. Brad owned a delicatessen, and each year he sponsored a hole at the annual police golf outing. The outing was held to help out needy families in the community by sending baskets of food at Thanksgiving. Not only did he support the charitable event by kicking in the hundred collars as a sponsor for one of the eighteen holes, he cooked a few dozen turkeys in his ovens at the deli each year. He also prepared the mashed potatoes, stuffing, and gravy.

"Thanks for returning my call. I would like to stop by tomorrow evening with my son, Billy. We have something we would like to discuss. Hopefully, your children will be at home."

"Sure thing, come by after dinner."

"How about around eight o'clock? Is that okay?"

"See you then."

The men said their goodbyes and hung up.

Mr. Duncan knew what the meeting was about. He discussed it with his wife; purposefully, he did not talk to his children because he did not want them to be upset.

Promptly at 8:00 p.m. on Monday, Brad Phillips rang the doorbell. Billy, who was nervously pacing back and forth like a baseball runner on first base trying to steal second, was at his side. After they were escorted into the living room and hellos were passed around, the Duncan children were called from their work desks in the basement where they were finishing their homework. Nanny, in her usual position, overseeing the daily homework ritual, climbed the stairs too. Sensing the hostility in the air, she slithered along at Robby's side with her ears at half-mast, alert to the truculent tension in the usually calm household.

Mr. Phillips and Billy stood and the Duncan family seated themselves; the children each huddled on either side of their mother. Nanny sat attentively at Robby's feet, sitting at attention, motionless, like a still life painting of ripening and speckled bananas on a plate.

Mr. Phillips, standing stiffly and facing the family, began, "Billy has been thinking about his past actions, and he has something he would like to say to the family."

Billy shuffled his feet with guilt hanging on him like a suit of stolen clothes, and he said, "I have been saying mean things to Robby and Gina." He sniffled and held back tears as he continued, "I will never do it again. I-I-I am so sorry, and I hope you accept my apology."

After writing down what he was going to say and rehearsing for hours, the delivery was choppy yet sincere.

Mr. Duncan looked at the children and asked them if they accepted the apology. Robby quickly said yes, and Gina buried her head into the side of her mother's dress.

The Duncan parents smiled at Billy, who felt as if a hundred-pound weight had been lifted off his chest.

Mrs. Duncan went and hugged Billy, saying, "My mother always said that forgiveness was easier to give then to ask for."

With Gina still clinging to her, she retreated to the kitchen and came back with brownies she baked earlier that day. Robby and Billy had milk and brownies as Gina continued to cling to her mother's side, sobbing silently.

After good nights were said, the Phillips left the Duncan home.

Mr. Phillips remarked on the way down the front steps, "That wasn't so very hard, was it, Billy?"

"No, it really wasn't as difficult as I thought it would be, but boy, I was very scared!"

A partial moon skidded across the sky as they drove home. Billy learned that no matter how bad things might seem, there was always room for a second chance, or at the very least, a chance for forgiveness. As far as delivering the apology, Mr. Phillips told his son that many times thinking about doing something, such as apologizing for past errors, was even harder than doing it.

As they began their journey, the tension between Billy and his dad could have been cut with a knife; but as they drove back into their driveway, the air had been filtered into a newfound breath of respect. They were smiling as they entered their home and obviously saddled with success from their visit. Hugs and kisses were passed all around, and to Billy's surprise, he embraced his sister for the first time. It seemed that familial love could blossom even in a barren family member with a little work once weeds were plucked. A little fertilizer mixture of understanding, concern, and caring was all that was needed.

Although it took action, or lack of action, on Billy's part, the Duncan children believed more pleasant days at both school and dancing classes were in their futures.

Mrs. Duncan was a firm believer that when you make mistakes, you have the courage to begin a fresh start just as things were looking the gloomiest. She knew that her son received a valuable life message from the conflict, and hopefully, everyone would see a new beginning for Billy Phillips. It would take time for Gina to appreciate the necessity to ask for forgiveness and then try again.

Liz Duncan kept this positive attitude about never giving up at work and did her best to instill it in her children. If she failed to sell a specific home to a customer, she would show another home and then another one until she succeeded. If her children did not do too well on a test at school, they were taught to redouble their efforts for the next test and continue to apply themselves.

A current song, with which Liz made sure the children were familiar, said it as well as it could be put. We all made mistakes, but "pick yourself up and try again." And if you fail a second time, "pick yourself up and try again." Unfortunately, the artist who popularized this song, Aaliyah, had just died in an airplane crash. She and eight others perished in an overloaded Cessna 402 on August 25, 2001. She was only twenty-two years old and had just finished filming a music video for her hit single, "Rock the Boat." Upon investigation, it was discovered that the pilot was on drugs and had alcohol in his system.

Aaliyah's signature song about trying again and then again and still again if necessary was life's foundation her parents cemented into her at an early age, and Liz Duncan was determined to imbue her children with the truth and reward of this credo. Absolutely nothing is able to hold you back from taking a stab at another chance to right a wrong or be successful in life.

12

ALTHOUGH LIZ FELT very uncomfortable letting Robby play basketball at Deergrove School, her husband insisted he be allowed to lead a normal life despite his problem. Instructed to mask his attached fingers with tape by his mom, Robby ignored this demand and never gave a second thought to his deformity as he dribbled, passed, and shot, knowing from the past that any attempt at hiding his hand only brought attention to it. He had twenty-twenty vision because of his contact lenses, and he developed an accurate outside jump shot that was guided by the joined fingers of his right hand. The swish of the net as the ball tickled the twine, passing though the orange cylinder, was a euphoric sound to his ears.

He would give-and-go by passing the ball to the much-taller Billy Phillips, now a close friend, who played the center position on the team. Being very quick and adept at changing direction or picking his defensive man off on another teammate, he would streak toward the hoop and receive a return pass from Billy. His layups and short hook shots that followed were Robby's signature moves on the court. Coach Robinson, who watched Robby develop while coaching the eighth-grade team, compared Robby to a young reincarnation of John Havelchek, the speedy star from bygone Celtic basketball days, who would outhustle his opponents and score at will while cutting to the goal.

Robby averaged fourteen points a game during his season as captain of the team. His team was much prouder of his average number of assists, a record ten passes responsible for the scoring of others per contest. Robby, like all good team players, did not care about his statistics. When they finished the season with a twelve wins and two loses record, *Long Island Newsday* did a write-up on the team in general and Robby in particular.

Previously, a picture of Robby making a left-handed layup over a much-taller player appeared with a narrative, praising him and his efforts in the newspaper. Mr. Duncan contacted the paper for the original of the article, and it was framed and hung in the hallway outside Robby's bedroom. A copy proudly graced his police locker at the downtown station house.

Deergrove Has a Sure Winner

For the second time this season, Deergrove outlasted their next-door neighbor, Ocean Pines, in a sixth-grade contest on the hardwood floor. Trailing by two points with only eight seconds to play, Robby Duncan flashed to the hoop and was fouled as he attempted a layup. With ice in his veins, he made both of his free throws to move the game into overtime with the score knotted at forty points apiece. During the extra frame, Robby took over, scoring six of the seven points to lead his team to a 47 to 44 victory. Duncan finished with eighteen points to lead all scorers, eleven assists, and seven rebounds. His teammates carried their captain from their home court as the full-to-capacity gym erupted in applause.

The next school year, when Robby was in seventh grade, he was a starting guard on the eighth-grade team. Now playing for Coach Robinson and a year younger than everyone else on the team, he practiced in the gymnasium every day both before and after school.

As his reputation as a "gym rat" grew, he did also! Now five feet eleven inches tall, he was the second tallest player on the team.

Billy Phillips, who was now his best friend, was over six feet tall. The two boys were inseparable as they attended classes throughout the school, and they hung-out together after the final bell rang to end the school day.

Robby was moved to a forward position where he took control of the game as a swingman, alternately handling the ball like a guard and much of the time working as a forward. If he wasn't distributing the ball, he was receiving it for his jump shot. His outside shot had remarkable range; he scored over 60 percent of the time when ten feet or farther away from the backboard. As he gracefully glided and then hung in the air before he released the ball, he took on the appearance of a cloud billowing out of reach of his bewildered defenders.

13

GINA WAS NEVER happier or more confident then when she was taking dancing lessons or performing at recitals. However, away from the safety of dance or her home, she felt like she was constantly surrounded by stale air billowing with waves of unrest. Name-calling directed at her and her brother that she continually experienced at an early age was like a wound that would not heal! An exception was when she was nestled in the safety net of her parents and proudly watching Robby perform on the basketball court.

The cheerleaders, middle-school girls in the sixth through eighth grades, cheered for the football and basketball teams at Deergrove. While Robby was starring on the court, Gina dreamed of one day joining the ranks of the cheerleaders. Although she had the athletic skills, she lacked confidence in social settings. Performing in the cloistered setting of dancing school and allowing that self-assurance to propel and support her during public performances was very different than spending the extra time at school necessary to make the cheerleading squad. School was too riddled with bad memories, and most days she felt like an outcast, attending classes in a withdrawn state of anxiety. Her grades were marginal, and if she was called on in class to answer a question, she responded in such a low voice the teacher as well students a couple of rows away were unable to hear her reply.

Since she was able to talk and interact with those around her, Gina loved to play games. Her earliest happy childhood memories revolved around Chutes and Ladders, Trouble, and Sorry. Additionally, she also loved playing card games: Old Maid and Go Fish. Many Saturdays were spent in her basement, playing these games and Twister with the twin sisters who lived next door. Sarah and Alisa Harrison were Gina's playmates, and the three girls especially enjoyed having Robby spin the dial and call out the colors for hand and foot placement in the green, yellow, blue, and red-colored circles of Twister. Unfortunately, the friendship between Gina and the twins was short-lived because the children moved away when they were six and a half years old. Mr. Harrison's job necessitated a transfer to the Midwest. When very young children are separated from friends, the feeling of loss and loneliness may have a debilitating effect on them. In Gina's case, the loss was further compounded because her favorite aunt, Mrs. Duncan's sister, who recently married, moved out of Gina's life with her husband to Chicago, Illinois. Gina somehow felt there was something wrong with her which caused the separations. Fortunately, Robby and her mom were there to fill the void of companionship, if only partially. The board game of Connect Four and card game UNO helped rekindle her love of games and competitive spirit. However, she felt empty at loss of close personal contact with friends, and these feelings of detachment caused her to involuntarily put up walls of indifference toward others.

Gina entered the fourth grade in her usual troubled state, consciously doing her best to blend in with her classmates. Trying not to call attention to herself, she did just that! As usual, rising apprehension during personal interaction with others caused her tear ducts to spit droplets into her eyes, causing her to blink at her surroundings through vision much like through the reflection of a foggy mirror after a hot shower.

Fortunately for Gina, she entered the fifth-grade class of Ms. Sullivan, who was a first-year teacher who loved to play games with her students. "Play as you learn and grow," was the class motto. It was splashed above the chalkboard in the front of the room, and at every opportunity Ms. Sullivan involved the children in learning games.

Gina started to peek her head out of her shell during math games wherein the students kept a scorecard on themselves to keep track of the number of addition, multiplication, or division examples they finished during the forty minutes allotted to arithmetic. After the daily exercises were completed, the teacher did the calculations on the board, and the children corrected their own work. You scored an A on the math game by completing the questions, and only the individual students knew how many problems they had to correct because of errors. In this nonthreatening environment, Gina took pride in learning for the first time.

When it was time for learning grammar, students took out his or her "ah" card. This was an index card on which they kept track of their own stuttering and hesitations. When called upon, if you stammered or came out with an "ah," "um," or "like," you had to put a tick mark on their card. If you did not speak loudly enough to be heard across the room, you also earned a tick mark on your card. In order to play the game, you had to speak up and answer questions. Gina continued to break out of her self-imposed isolation and found she enjoyed the challenging game of speaking clearly, and for the first time, her fellow classmates clearly heard her voice, which became less choppy and more distinct during the daily grammar lessons.

Two months into the year, Ms. Sullivan told the students to put away their "ah" cards. She said she would sock the next person who came out with a nervous utterance. When Henry Jackson, who was considered the smartest child in the class, slipped and said, "An adverb is, um, similar to an, ah, adjective, except it modifies a verb," he was socked by his teacher. A pair of crew socks was ceremoniously tossed on his desk. The children had a good laugh at the "Sock It to Me" game. When another student came out with a speaking error, Henry was told to put the socks on his desk. The children enjoyed this game, especially when four or five pairs of socks were being tossed from desk to desk.

The object of the game was to let it die on its own because it could no longer be played in the classroom. Confidence in grammar and speaking flourished, and the children all won at the game. Ms.

Sullivan retired her jogging socks to her dresser drawer, where they would sit until next year's fifth-grade class arrived.

With the comet of computers striking Earth, being a good speller was a lost art that seemed to have gone the way of the dinosaur. Reasoning was that spell-check was a just a click away, so why learn how to spell?

Ms. Sullivan was very insistent that her students be able to spell as well as know how to correctly use their vocabulary words in sentences. The game of Sparkle was used to promote good spelling and word usage; at week's end, it was a tool to review the spelling and vocabulary words for the week. Students would line up around the classroom, and a word would be given to the first student. In turn, the word was passed along the line of students as they each gave the next letter to spell the word. When an error was made, the student must sit down, and the game continued until the spelling was complete. The next student after the spelled word was correctly spelled said "Sparkle." The game continued through the spelling and vocabulary review session. After spelling the words correctly, all students who misspelled a word rejoined the lined-up students, and the words were spelled again, but instead of saying "Sparkle," the next student after the word was correctly spelled gave the definition of the word. The game continued by moving on to antonyms and then by making up a sentence by using the word. Gina loved playing "Sparkle," and all students looked forward to the end of each week when they would play the game.

Gina's love of games was transformed to a love of learning in Ms. Sullivan's class. Unfortunately, when she was not in her classroom, Gina again regressed into her usual melancholic mood.

14

COACH ROBINSON ALWAYS seemed to have a "special project" boy on his eighth-grade basketball team. He believed all children were inherently good and that the reason they floundered in school or were showing signs of aberrant social behavior was because they knew no better. Victor Larson was an eighth-grade student who fit this mold. Victor always seemed to have a chip on his shoulder and be moments away from boiling over and seething with anger at someone or something. This was especially evident during games when his team was behind. He was a blamer; if things were not going well, it was the fault of the referees, his teammates, or the equipment. He was not above yelling at a referee when he didn't like a call, and he sulked and hung his head when a foul was called on him.

Victor's dad left his mom when he was four years old. He had an older sister, Lara, along with his younger brother, Sammy. Mrs. Larson struggled to raise the three children and provide them with all the tools they would need to be successful in life. Many of the children in and around the middle-class neighborhood of Deergrove came from broken homes, so the Larson family was not atypical. With an absentee father, they were forced to live with Mrs. Larson's parents. Their father did not provide child support, and Lilly Larson worked as a waitress at the Deergrove Diner to provide for her children. She would kick in whatever money she could to help her parents, who were just getting by on social security, with household expenses.

Although Lilly's daughter never seemed to cause a problem, the household seemed to be in constant turmoil because of Victor and Sammy's behavior. At the age of seven, Victor would talk back to the adults in the home, and he would come and go as he pleased, breaking the family rule of letting his mom know where he was going, whom he was with, and the time he would return. And Sammy followed in the misplaced steps of his older brother.

Long Island, before sewer piping was run under the streets of the neighborhoods to allow rain runoff an escape route to the surrounding waters was, and still is, snaked with creeks. These aqueducts were designed into the township plans before it became common practice to dig water basins at periodic intervals into the landscape. Long Island was so flat, without a means for the precipitation's release or a way for it to pool in man-made reservoirs, indoor swimming pools in the basements were a common occurrence. The creeks were filled with sand and wound their way throughout the town of Deergrove. Bridges over the rarely wet tributaries allowed traffic to pass from one part of the town to another; and pedestrian crossovers dotted the suburban landscape. The spaces under the pedestrian overpasses as well as places under the vehicular bridges were the hangout spots for the youth of the town.

Mostly harmless gangs of kids claimed a certain crossover as a meeting place of their own, and territoriality was rarely a problem. The gang that Victor Larson belonged to was the Nightcrawlers, or the Crawlers for short. The guys, never girls, on the surrounding blocks where they lived crawled from the dried-up creek into a four-foot-wide tunnel and traveled over two hundred feet to where the tunnel opened up into an eight-by-eight-foot "room" under a manhole cover. From their meeting room other concrete pipes, now only three and a half feet wide, led to water drainage openings in the curbs throughout the town. Based on the tight quarters and the necessity to gasp for the limited amount of oxygen when occupied by a number of Crawlers, the meeting place was called the Coffin by all gang members. These underground passageways, branching off from the Coffin, gave the explorers countless hours of adventure as they crawled under the town of Deergrove.

The Nightcrawlers kept a stash of candles and matches in their underground retreat. As initiation to the club, new gang members had to crawl to the meeting room alone and without any light. Flashlights and lit candles were not allowed until this solo crawl was accomplished. This kept the younger and "scaredy cat" kids from being able to join. Many times a pledge traveled only about fifteen feet and became so frightened he had to back out (a disgraceful word) crying, to be greeted by the jeering and taunts of the Crawlers' club members. This happened to Victor the first three times he tried to make the petrifying journey. For over two months, he was teased by other club members who called him a "Back Outer."

Most days after school, the Nightcrawlers met in their sub-terranean cement clubhouse, smoking cigarettes that they snitched from their parents. Even the youngest and most newly accepted Nightcrawler smoked in the meeting room. If a resident of the town happened by the manhole cover over the Coffin when a meeting was being held, walking a dog or simply while going for a stroll, puffs of smoke might be seen escaping from the holes used to pry the cover off with a crowbar. Nothing was ever thought of these smoke signals, as it was commonly believed that sewer gas had to escape from the manhole-cover openings.

An assortment of kneepads used by Long Island Lighting Company (LILCO) employees when they worked under ground and on their knees had found their way to the stash kept in the Coffin. The more-experienced Crawlers used these when they went for long labyrinth excursions in their serpentine underground world.

On his fourth try and at the age of seven, Victor passed his initiation and became a member of the Nightcrawlers. The incentive to join was not just the prestige of saying you were a member but also included the added celebrity of everyone knowing you were able to smoke. If a younger sibling of a Crawler or any Back Outer was caught smoking by a gang member, he would be taken to his parents; they were told about the smoking! Everyone knew that if the ratted-out child mentioned that a club member smoked, they would be shunned and never again allowed to try the lonely inductive and much-desired crawl. Boys who had not made the grade were referred to as Littleuns. Club members put a "Little" before their name and an "ie" after it. So when Victor proudly crawled to the inner gathering sanctum alone, not only could he smoke, he went from being called "Little Vicie" to "Victor"!

Victor was surprised when he first saw the glory of the meeting place by candlelight, with three wooden milk crates stacked on top of each other in the center of the sacred room. Valuables, to include candles, matches, kneepads, and cigarettes were kept in the middle or top milk box. This was because the anchor or lower box was often flooded when it rained. Bricks in the bottom box kept the treasures above from washing away if a particularly heavy downpour occurred. Victor spent countless hours being counseled about how to act the first time he attempted to smoke. He was warned to take it easy the first few times and not rush to inhale the forbidden chemicals.

On the day he was indoctrinated and stopped being called a Back Outer and Little Vicie, Victor sat, squatting with a Marlboro between his fingers with the Crawlers gathered around him in the hallowed chamber. As part of the ceremony, the first-time smoker had to light his cigarette all by himself. Mimicking older club members, Victor pressed the sulfur part of the match against the striking pad with the index finger of his left hand as he pulled the matchstick out with his right hand. Looking like a forgotten actor in a long-ago black-and-white movie, he crouched with the cigarette perched in his mouth. When he tugged on the match, the red-colored tip went up in flames and stuck to the tip of his finger. Now he was a Crawler, and he knew he couldn't cry, so he yipped in pain a few times as he instinctively brushed the burning match tip from his finger. This first cigarette, his initiation smoke, fell into the moist dirt of the venerated chamber floor of the Coffin. After a few moments, he tried again. On the second try, he lit the now dirty and damp cigarette. During the ritual smoking instruction, he was told to just draw a little smoke into his mouth and blow it out.

Although he knew not to breathe in, Victor drew the poisonous fumes into his lungs, and he coughed like he never had before.

Bravely, he tried again and inhaled, causing him to have a ferocious reaction of hacking and spitting. Embarrassed, he continued, as his pallor turned a shade of yellow green, and he threw up the ham sandwich and Twinkies he had for lunch a few hours earlier. Although it was common to see a new smoker puking in the Coffin, he recovered rather quickly and came out with a stream of curse words that made all present feel that he really belonged.

Another well-publicized advantage to being a Crawler was that you could curse. Anybody with an "ie" after their name and Little or Lil before it was simply too young to curse; finally, after making the solo crawl, you were now a man and able to put a stream of blasphemous words together. If a Back Outer used bad language, the Crawlers would look at him as if he had two heads. More than one Lil was escorted to his mother by a Crawler and forced to own up to cursing comments that were verbalized in the presence of a full-fledged, foulmouthed club member. Older brothers even ratted out their younger siblings, letting parents know they used foul language.

Secretive handshakes and greetings support the need of members of many groups to feel set apart from those around them, and Crawlers were no different. They had a great desire to feel special, if not better, than others. While in school, the Crawlers always acknowledged another member of the group. When they passed each other in the hallways, entered a class together, or made eye contact during any lesson, they would mimic how they would hold a hand when they inched their way through the underground tunnels. Flattening out their right hand, waist high, with wrist bent upward and then extending it in a downward manner accomplished this greeting. In Deergrove School, the other students labeled the Crawlers "bad kids."

By the time Victor Larson was nine, he was considered the worst of the worst.

15

ALONG WITH SWITCHING classes for different subjects, the students at Deergrove were given lockers in the sixth grade. All students with the exception of Gina looked forward to this rite of passage. Not only did you get a few minutes to go to your next classroom, if you were well organized with your books for the next period, you could avoid stopping at your locker and get a drink of water on your way down the hall. Gina planned her day well, but her goal was to never stop at the water fountains; it was to blend in with the other students and become invisible on her way to the next lesson. At times, she walked in an almost zombielike state as she made her way to the next classroom. She would not flip the switch that dialed her back to normalcy until she was seated in her next class.

Gina always dreaded the hectic time at the end of the day after the dismissal bell rang. After pouncing on their lockers to deposit books and pick out those necessary for the night's homework, the hallways would be empty of students in a matter of moments. Gina always hung back after social studies, her last class of the day, so she could enjoy the solitude of opening her locker and methodically retrieve the books she would need for the evening or weekend. After exiting the main entrance, she would meet her mother who was waiting in the parking lot to drive her home.

During the second week of classes, on a Thursday, Gina found a note in her locker that must have been slipped in through the small slotted openings in the metal door. It said, "Gina, welcome to the sixth grade, you freak show." Because she did not come out of the school building to go home, Mrs. Duncan entered and went into the principal's office. Together they walked down the hallway and found Gina balled up on the floor, sobbing with the note in her hand.

Rushing toward her daughter, Mrs. Duncan pleaded, "What's the matter, Gina? What happened?"

Gina babbled, "Look, look," as she held the neatly typed note out for her mother to see.

Principal Scott tried to calm Mrs. Duncan, who had tears uncontrollably cascading down her cheeks as she knelt over and held her child.

"Mrs. Duncan, we will get to the bottom of this! I'm so sorry this happened. I assure you we will find out who typed that terrible note."

Still sobbing, Gina left the building with her mother to go home. The note was left with Mrs. Scott.

Investigation into the incident began the next day; meanwhile, it was decided that the unpleasant event would not be publicized. Based on her many years of experience and knowing children well—all people, especially children, cannot keep a secret—Principal Clark was confident that the author who typed the note would soon be discovered. A secret shared is a secret no longer. If more than one person knows something, especially if that knowledge is humiliating toward another, much like an off-color joke, it will be passed around among friends and acquaintances. This was no exception!

The cafeteria monitoring staff was told to keep their eyes and ears open to rumors and whispers being spread during the lunch period. The day after the incident was Friday, and Gina did not go to school. She was too upset, and Mrs. Duncan kept her home and did her best to comfort her during the day.

Mark Rollins, a friend of Victor Larson's younger brother, Sammy, typed out the message during tying class. Everyone knew how sensitive Gina was, and Mark believed he would be elevated in the eyes of his friends if he carried on the evil tradition and did something to hurt the introverted child.

Sitting at the lunch table the very next day with Sammy Larson, Mark discussed the absence of Gina from school. Previously, Mark had shared knowledge of the inflammatory note with Sammy, who laughed and commented to him that whatever such a crazy kid got she had coming to her. After Sammy disclosed the secret to his older brother by pinky-swearing, information spread around the school like germs during the cold season. Most tables were busy buzzing with the business about the locker incident. This was not lost on a teacher's aide who was present and helping to keep order in the cafeteria. Immediately after the lunch period, as instructed, she went and discussed what she had heard with Principal Alexis Clark.

Both Mark Rollins and Sammy Larson were in the same mathematics class after lunch. Shortly after the period began, Sammy was called down to the principal's office. Mrs. Clark kept him squirming in a chair outside her office for over five minutes before calling him to speak with her. Unsure if Sammy wrote the note, she wanted him to confess to all he knew.

"There is a nasty rumor going around that you were involved in an incident that occurred yesterday in school," Principal Clark began. She continued, "I know what happened, and I believe you do also. Tell me all you know about it!"

Sammy, looking as if his hands were caught in the cookie jar, hung his head and said, "I didn't do nothing."

"I didn't say that you did. However, I have been told quite a bit about what happened and your possible involvement."

"I swear I didn't do nothing. Some of the kids have been talking about why Gina Duncan is not in school today, and my brother and me ain't involved."

Meanwhile, Mark Rollins was paged to come to the nurse's office, where he paced in front of Nurse Gottlieb, trying to hide behind a conscientious-student look, out of sight of Sammy who was still behind closed doors with the principal.

Mark began, "I'm not sick, why am I here?"

"Because Sammy is in with Mrs. Clark, and you are next to go in and talk with her."

Turning almost as red as the framed picture of the apples on the wall, Mark began to sweat bullets of perspiration that beaded on his forehead and trickled down his shirt from his armpits. He leaned forward as tense as an arrow set in a bowstring, thinking he would be sick.

Sammy remained tight-lipped and would not tell Mrs. Clark what he knew about the incident. He was dismissed after ten more minutes of denials and was allowed to return to class. Mark, laced as tightly with guilt as were his sneakers, was then ushered into the principal's office.

"Do you know why you are here?" asked Principal Clark. "I have just had a long discussion with Sammy about the incident involving Gina Duncan that occurred yesterday. Tell me about your participation, and I want the truth! I already know about it and want to hear your side of the story."

"I did it, I'm sorry. Please don't tell my father. He will kill me!"

"That can't be avoided. It is my responsibility to let your parents know what you did. You will have to explain to them the why! It was a very mean thing to do. You have caused a lot of trouble for Gina and her family. There are penalties for such action, and you will have to suffer the consequences."

Mrs. Clark had Mark wait outside her office while she called his mother at her place of employment. Mrs. Rollins left work and picked up her son twenty minutes later. She and Mark sat with the principal as he babbled on about typing the note and slipping it into Gina's locker. His punishment was that he would be suspended from school for a week. Crying, he was taken home by his mother, and he would have to face the wrath of both of his parents.

The Principal then called Mrs. Duncan and explained that the author of the note was discovered. Keeping confidentiality, she simply explained that the boy who wrote the note confessed and that for her part, the incident was over. After asking how Gina felt, she hung up the phone, knowing one of her most unpleasant but necessary duties was now behind her. Mrs. Duncan was very thankful, and she told Principal Clark how satisfied she was that the culprit had been caught.

The weekend in both the Duncan and especially in the Rollins households was long and not too pleasant.

Gina discussed Robby's problem and how it affected her in school with her parents. Somehow, she felt ashamed and knew she could not hide her fear and disappointment with the cards she had been dealt in life. It wasn't her fault, it wasn't Robby's fault, and wasn't her parents' fault that some of the students could be so cruel.

Mrs. Duncan spoke of forgiveness as she told her daughter that some children just didn't think about the consequences of their actions and how much they could hurt others.

Mr. Duncan added, "When something like this happens, you can either forgive or hold a grudge. And holding on to bitterness only hurts the person who must carry it around."

Gina said, "I know, Dad, but it is very hard, but I will try to do my best not to hate anyone."

Mrs. Duncan added, "Hate is like a cancer that spreads throughout your body. It must be cut out by understanding, or it will only hurt you and spread to others around you."

Gina returned to school on Monday, and she resumed her in-and-out-again disappearing act as she made her way through the school day.

For his part, Mark Rollins had a terrible week at home while he was suspended. He was not allowed to leave the house at all, except to take out the garbage. His mother had to pick up his homework and his books daily after school. After serving his at-home suspension, he returned to school. Not knowing how to act, he returned at first feeling sorrow and humiliation. This quickly changed as he was greeted as a hero by his friends. Once again, he assumed his chosen behavior of being a bully and showing no respect for anyone but himself and his friends.

Mr. and Mrs. Rollins let life get in the way, and they, too, allowed Mark to once again spiral down on his self-destructive path of delinquency.

16

LEADERSHIP IS A quality that separates "gifted" persons from others. There are many examples of malignant members of society who have risen to have others blindly follow. Maybe there is a hollow place in many people that they want filled with acceptance by following the lead of others, whether the leaders have earned their respect and are a positive force or if their conduct clashes with the usual societal norms. This is especially true of young children as they strive to fit their round personalities into the square pegs of peer relationships. Just as cream rises to the top, fetid materials sometimes form a filthy film on the surface of still pond water.

When Billy Phillips, who was the unofficial leader of the Crawlers, was awakened to his personality flaws because of the way he treated the Duncan children and others, he quit the club. A void was felt in the Crawlers after this negative leader quit. Actually, he didn't resign; he just stopped meeting and crawling and no longer associated with members of the group. This antisocial group cried for an antisocial leader, and Victor Larson floated to the surface and was accepted as Billy's replacement.

Just as charitable and caring personalities are further developed by kindness and a realization of adding to the common good, Victor's negative character flaws spread over him much like poison ivy was spread by scratching. Close daily contact with other group members in the Coffin caused Victor's caustic contagion to further spread to other Crawlers. Three eight-year-olds were especially receptive to Victor's diseased personality: Tommy Johnson and the twin brothers Louis and Larry Burris.

The Crawlers always seemed to be short on money. If there were plenty of candles, there were not enough snacks. And as far as smoking was concerned, after being initiated into the club, picking up half-smoked butts found on the street was beneath someone who braved the tunnels alone and in the dark. But where to get money? Although not the oldest, the gang looked to Fat Bobby and Tommy Johnson for the answer, as they seemed to be jockeying to take more of a leadership role recently.

Fat Bobby devised an ingenious plan after polling the subterranean audience as to their need for money one day.

"We don't want to lift the money from our mothers' pocketbooks or take it off our fathers' dressers," Fat Bobby told the guys ruefully. "I've tried that and had my butt beaten so I could hardly crawl."

Tommy said, "Maybe we can do odd jobs around the house and put our allowance money together so we can buy what we need."

There were quite a few boys who everyone knew would not kick in, and they would spend their money on snacks and sodas at the candy store for themselves only.

"What about dues?" asked Ralph. He was a Crawler who had repeatedly tried to move up in the crawling hierarchy but knew he would never be taken seriously because he always seemed to be mooching off other club members.

Dues, huh, that's an idea that might work. And if a member does not pay their dues, what do we do with them, not allow them to crawl? thought Bobby to himself.

Victor took control and said, "Dues could be twenty-five or thirty-five cents a man per week, but then we would need someone to keep track of who paid and who didn't. Does anyone want to volunteer?"

Three of the newest members raised their hands. Sal, Matt, and Alex were all not even eight years old, and the more-senior members thought they could just about count at their age; how on earth, or under earth, could they handle such an important responsibility?

Victor decided, "Every Friday after school, each of us will put whatever change we can in a collection bucket. You can get the money anywhere or any way you can. If we can each come up with enough money to buy all our necessities, this should work out just fine. This doesn't mean you shouldn't lift candles, matches, candy, and cigarettes from stores or from home. Payment can be the cost of items rather than the money to buy them. Does everyone agree?"

When a vote was asked for, or agreement sought, each member got on his hands and knees to vote yes and simply stayed in the squatting position if they voted no. All Crawlers present, except Ralph, who stayed in the squatting position, got in the crawl position, and the vote was twelve to one that they would try Victor's plan.

Victor looked at Ralph, the lone dissenter, and said, "Hey, are you with us or not?"

Ralph took a three-point stance, two knees and one hand. The gang always accepted a three-point vote by Ralph as affirmative as long as two knees where on the ground, knowing he seemed to always be complaining about a hurt left arm.

Victor, the Burris twins, and Fat Bobby advanced an idea they had been thinking about for the past couple days. They even tried it to make sure it would work. They pushed a piece of cloth up the coin return slot of a candy machine at school and used a wire clothes hanger which they bent to act as a hook to pull it out. Change for a sale was dispensed in the return slot. Each time they did this, they ended up with twenty cents or more.

Ralph, trying to get into the good graces of Victor, said, "So what, that's not a lot of money!" sneering at Bobby.

Fat Bobby took this personally and said, "So what, sew buttons on your old man's trousers. You would think you were made of money. You are the cheapest member of the club."

Ralph, who was two years younger and fifteen pounds lighter than Fat Bobby, jumped at him, and they rolled around for two minutes on the dirty floor of the Coffin. There was dirt, but no blood, all over each boy as they were separated. Ralph knew he was wrong and cried; he was forced to apologize. When he said, "I am sorry," he had his fingers crossed, and although nobody saw this legitimate and very acceptable move, everyone knew he didn't mean it.

Victor continued by asking each boy what kind of vending machines there were in town and how many of them needed exact change. A list was compiled which included seven soda machines, four dispensers of soap and bleach in each of the two laundromats, a machine for pens and rabbit feet in the candy store, and three candy machines in the school.

Victor asserted himself, "If we divide up all the machines that give change in town and work in teams of twos, one lookout and one pushing a rag up the change slot, we can clean up. We won't ever have to worry about having enough cigarettes, candles, or snacks again."

The boys broke into two-man teams, with Fat Bobby and Ralph not on the same team and not because they had just gotten into a fight. It was decided by a vote of ten to two—as leader, Victor abstained from voting—with all but Bobby and Ralph getting on their hands and knees that anyone who fought with another member or was overweight could only act as a lookout man.

The next day the plan was put into motion. Twosomes paired off after school, and they each worked one machine. Sal and Matt, the two youngest boys, were assigned as partners to Victor and Larry. Larry peddled his bicycle up to the Coke machine outside the hardware store, and while Sal kept lookout so no one in the store could see him, he shoved a napkin up the change return with a pencil. As the boys jumped back on their bikes, Sal's chest was pounding so hard he thought his heart may jump out in front of him, and he would then run it over. Although Larry felt an adrenaline rush, he just smiled at his young protégé as they peddled from State Street and down Deergrove Avenue. They drove past the candy store, on the other side of the street, and up to the laundromat where Victor had just plugged the coin return of the three machines that dispensed little packets of laundry detergent and bleach as Matt was standing at the doorway to make sure no customers were about to enter. The two young lookouts giggled as they bragged about their newfound notoriety. Tom could hardly catch his breath, and Matt hid the fact that he peed his pants during their first big caper.

By the end of three days, the booty added up to $6.30 in coin and two slugs. And the money kept rolling in! For over two months there was never a problem, and the Crawlers had all the money they needed. That was until residents started complaining about the vending machines. When a couple boys were caught suspiciously hanging out around places of business with tissues and handkerchiefs in their pockets, along with pockets of change, they were taken to the police station, and their parents were called. After confessing and having a few Crawlers grounded, the gang decided to abandon the strategy.

The Crawlers always hung out together in the hallways of school, in the cafeteria, and after three o'clock under the bridge near the entrance tunnel to their underground hideaway. They would routinely call other children names and throw things at them as they passed by. Like a pack of hyenas that focused on the weakest member of a herd, they looked for and found their prey, walking alone and isolated from their friends. And Gina was one of the weakest.

17

MRS. DUNCAN PICKED up Gina after school every day except when she was able to walk home with her older brother. Although Gina had a very rough time interacting with her peers, each Friday she crossed over the creek that separated her house from the school accompanied by Robby and a few of the kids who played with him on the eighth-grade basketball team. The walk home took less than ten minutes. Basketball games were held on Fridays; therefore, there was no practice after school on the day of a game, and Robby was happy to walk with his sister. A year behind her brother, in the sixth grade, she shuffled along, only half listening to the conversation of the guys, which usually revolved around sports and girls. Billy Phillips, towering over the pack, looked forward to walking with Gina. His past bravado and mean streak had softened into a much milder manner, and past hostility gave way to affectionate feelings toward Gina.

This Friday there was a very important home game against Ocean Pines, archrivals of the Deergrove Knights. The last forty minutes of the school day was dedicated to a pep rally at which the entire school gathered in the gym to watch the cheerleaders go through their routines and encourage support for the evening's hardwood contest. Special cheers were put together for the occasion. These would be replayed later during the game. To get the students involved in the new cheers, signs were made: "Say Good Knight to Ocean Pines" and "Ocean Pines Huskies Are Second Dogs."

Dressed in their cheerleading outfits, the young girls yelled, "Say good knight!" The screeching voices from the bleachers echoed back, "Say good knight!" This was followed by "To Ocean Pines." The gym resounded with "Say good knight, say good knight, say good night to Ocean Pines!" Similarly, "Ocean Pines Huskies, Ocean Pines Huskies, Ocean Pines Huskies are second dogs" bounced off the ceiling and gymnasium walls. Gina sat with her teacher, Ms. Robinson, and her sixth-grade classmates in the top row of seats. Outside the learning environment and game-playing security of the classroom, she was very uncomfortable as she longed to disappear in order to hide her uneasiness. She would convince herself that she was all alone and by herself where she did not have to interact with others. This defense mechanism was called upon whenever she felt herself drifting and out of place. She would think, *Get invisible, get invisible,* causing her to disappear from those around her, if only in her own mind. To her, the sounds of cheers and laughter that filled the gym seemed as nonsensical as the baying of horses and chattering of monkeys.

All students, except for the Crawlers, were in attendance. Knowing the school would be dismissed directly from the gym after the impromptu rally, the club members skipped out on the way to the pep rally, knowing they would not be missed. The other students streamed out of the gym at 3:00 p.m. and headed home for the weekend; almost all of them would reappear for the game against the Ocean Pines Huskies at 8:00 p.m.

A few minutes before dismissal, Coach Robinson addressed the students.

He spoke of the importance of the game later that evening and encouraged everyone to come out and cheer the Knights on to victory. He closed by asking the basketball players to stay behind. Instructing them to get into their gym uniforms, they went over the new plays he had put in place for the contest against Ocean Pines. Although they practiced well all week, he wanted one more run through to ensure all players knew their roles.

Team members went to the coach's office and called parents to let them know they would be late because of the spur of the moment practice session. Robby was unable to get in touch with his parents, but he knew they would not be concerned if he was late. He would explain later! Somehow, he forgot about his sister and that it was a day Mom would not be picking her up.

Gina waited outside for her brother, who never showed up to walk her home. After about twenty minutes, she walked from the rear of the school and gymnasium entrance to the front of the school. The doors were locked! Her usual state of anxiety was quickly replaced by panic as she ran back to the gym doors and pounded on them with her fists in hopes of being heard. Frustrated, she sat down on her book bag to try to decide what to do. As it began to drizzle, she started to cry as gray clouds rolled across the school grounds.

Robby arrived home after practice at 4:30 p.m. Because of the rain, Billy Phillips's mother drove him home. Mrs. Duncan drove up the driveway and entered the house a few minutes later.

When she entered the house, Robby asked, "Where is Gina?"

"I haven't seen her yet. What time did the two of you get home?"

"Didn't you pick her up after school?"

All of a sudden, like a slap of reality across his face, it hit him. It was Friday, and he was supposed to walk Gina home. The excitement of the pep rally and the last-minute decision to hold basketball practice confused him. Hanging his head in disbelief he replied, "Ma, I forgot about walking her home, there was a pep rally, coach called a practice, it is raining, Mrs. Phillips drove me home…"

When tragedy is shared and discussed, somehow it adds understanding and acceptance to a situation. When fear is shared, it is like a disease growing and multiplying as it feeds upon itself, passing from one vital organ to another. Although she knew he wouldn't be there, Mrs. Duncan called her husband at the police station. She left a message anyway, saying that she was out looking for Gina, who had not returned from school. Robby was told to wait at home for his father, and Mrs. Duncan ran out and got in her car to drive over to the school. Torrents of rain blanketed the streets like spilled ink as she flipped the wipers to high speed and made her way to the school.

Robby was sitting at the kitchen table when his father arrived home a few minutes later. Seeing only the back of his son, he asked,

"Ready for the big game? Where are Mom and Gina?" Not knowing the situation, he continued, "If pollywog is out in this weather, she may turn into a frog."

Seeing the blank look and pale face of his son, Mr. Duncan didn't have to ask to know there was something wrong.

"Mom just drove back to school. Gina did not come home after school, and we don't know where she is."

"It's Friday, didn't you walk her home?"

Robby began to cry, and his father tried to comfort him. When he had the facts, Mr. Duncan told Robby not to worry, that everything would be all right.

They were probably on their way home and would arrive any minute.

Maybe because he was a cop, maybe because it was just his personality; however, Mr. Duncan did not get too upset too easily. When his fellow police officers down at the precinct would think the worst outcome of a situation, he would tell them to stop "awfulizing." Mr. Duncan was not an "awfulizer"!

"She probably is at the Phillips house. Amy is in her dancing school class, and they probably went to Amy's house together."

Robby sobbed, "Mrs. Phillips drove me, us, Billy, me, and the guys home from practice today because it was raining. Amy, Amy was in the car with us. I can't figure out where Gina could be. She— she wasn't in the car with us, and Mr. Phillips is never home until after six o'clock, so she can't be at their home."

18

SITTING UNDER THE overhang of the gym door, Gina tried to keep dry. This became more difficult as the wind picked up, and the rain seemed to be almost coming down sideways. While having her face stung by the storm and fighting back sobs, she took deep breaths and tried to collect herself. She had walked home with her brother many times, and now she wrestled with the reality that she would have to make the trek alone for the first time. Putting one foot in front of the other, like the little engine that could she thought, *I think I can. I think I can, I think I can.* As she gained steam by picking up her pace, she continued, *I think I can. I think I can. I know I can. I know I can.*

Exiting the school grounds, she realized she left her book bag propped up against one of the back gym doors. It was Friday, and she would be returning for the basketball game; undoubtedly, she could get it later. Knowing it was protected from the rain and that she had all weekend to do her homework added little comfort to her troubled state of mind.

The Crawlers were squatting and smoking as they huddled together under the protection of a pedestrian crossover. Although the creek was only as wet as the ground around the overpass, the rain kept them from creeping into their desired meeting place, the Coffin. The entry tunnel still had a few inches of water in it from a prior rainstorm, and even the most hardened Crawler didn't want to end up soaked and cold after splashing through the water. Whenever they hung out under a bridge, someone was always assigned to be a lookout. This way, if on the unlikely chance that a parent of a Crawler happened by, they could ditch their cigarettes and possibly hide up under the bridge and not be seen.

Fat Bobby was the lookout, and he said to the group, "Kid coming at six o'clock."

Although this caused confusion for the very youngest members who could just about tell time, Crawlers used "o'clock talk" because it made them feel important as group members and helped add to their group identity.

"Probably one of them those basketball players. I am sure glad we got outta that pep rally. There was probably so much yelling and screaming it woulda woke up the dead," said Larry Burris.

Victor bumped Fat Bobby out to the way, saying, "Let's have a look-see." He continued, "It's that deformed kid's little sister, Gina. She is always slinking around with Robby and those jocks after school. Let's let her come close, and then we will have some fun with her."

As Gina approached the bridge to walk across and continue on her way home, the seven Crawlers present jumped out from under the bridge. They formed a circle around her.

"Where you going? You look like the wet rat that you are," chided Victor. He continued, "And where is Robby Four Fingers? Probably in the graveyard digging for his finger."

Matt was behind her, and he pushed Gina to the ground. Using her defensive mind game to make herself invisible, Gina stood straight up with mud dripping down her clothes. Unable to answer, even if she wanted to, she knew by speaking she would lose her ability not to be seen, so she refused to respond. Matt pushed her again, this time into Louis Burris, who pushed her into his twin brother, Larry. The chant of "freak family" was started by Victor and picked up by the other members of the group who continued to push her back and forth among themselves.

All but Fat Bobby joined in the name-calling and pushing. Bobby knew what it was like to be singled out because of his size, and although he felt he had to, he didn't want to take part in the cruelty. He was scared because he also knew that Mr. Duncan was a cop, and based on Robby's ability on the basketball court, he secretly admired him and the way he was able to rise above his deformity problem. Respect for Robby could not be verbalized; if a Crawler ever spoke positively about a non-Crawler, they would automatically be banished from the club and never again be greeted by the Crawler salute when passing by a club member at school. Bobby, like all youngsters, had a great need to belong, even if belonging meant he felt embarrassed at times by the actions of other group members. It is much easier to forgive your friends than to forgive those you do not know well. Maybe this is because you know you are like your friends, and if you cannot forgive your own actions, it is much more difficult to keep your sanity.

This was especially true when participating in mob activity as the Crawlers so often did.

After a few minutes and falling to the ground two more times, Gina refused to get up. She cradled her arms about herself in a fetal position while the clouds continued to unleash their fury upon her. Knowing she was now invisible and those around her could not harm her, she was determined to wait for the unseeing eyes to tire of hostility and leave her alone.

Leaving Gina in the mud, the band decided it was time for them to go home to their individual houses. Except for Bobby, they all left with no feelings of regret; it was just another day in the lives of the Crawlers. They skipped out of school early, cursed and smoked under the bridge, and harassed a non-club member who deserved what she got because she came from a family of deformity.

Gina laid on the ground for some time until she felt her visibility returning. After emerging from her unseen world, she always felt exhausted yet euphoric, and today was no different. Even the rainy chill that enveloped her body felt good!

She knew she would soon be home in her house and that her defense mechanisms had once again made it possible for her to survive in a hostile world.

Mrs. Duncan drove to Deergrove School and rang the doorbell at the main entrance. When there was no answer, she drove her minivan through the town, looking for her daughter. Meanwhile, Robby and his dad hopped into his pickup truck and searched for Gina. Circling the school, Robby noticed that Gina's book bag was lying against the gym door; stopping the truck, Mr. Duncan opened the tailgate and tossed it into the back of the truck.

Guilt because he forgot about his sister after the pep rally coursed through Robby, and he felt the pulsing pangs of suffering throbbing in his head.

"Dad, let me get out and walk home. I'll cut across the creek. Just maybe Gina walked home."

Mr. Duncan thought it was a good idea, but he was hesitant because the storm had intensified and was now accompanied by claps of thunder and bolts of lightning.

"Here, take my hooded coat and put it on over your coat. I'll drive around and meet you on the other side of the creek."

As Mr. Duncan pulled away, Robby walked across the baseball field and on the very well-worn path next to the creek. Although he knew it was almost impossible to be heard above the roar of the storm, he repeatedly shouted out Gina's name as he slugged his way through the rain and mud. Approaching the crossover, he saw Gina huddled under the bridge. Although caked in mud and soaked to the bone, she was not crying and didn't even appear to be upset.

Flipping in and out of her invisible world, she continued to take refuge within herself for protection. Her frightened demeanor was quickly replaced by a soft and calm expression at the sight of her brother.

"Robby, I had a terrible time. Victor and the mean kids wouldn't let me pass, and they pushed me down in the mud."

As Robby began to experience the beginnings of his release from the chains of guilt he had felt tightening about him, even the wail of the wind seemed to soften.

"Here, take off your jacket and put Dad's coat on. He is waiting for us on the other side of the bridge."

Through the blinding rain, Mr. Duncan saw his children cradled together under his coat as they made their way across the pedestrian crossing. He ran from the truck and put his arm around Gina, and after helping her into the truck, the three of them drove home.

"Are you okay, Apple Blossom? Does anything hurt?"

"No, I am just tired and cold."

When they arrived home, Mrs. Duncan saw the truck pulling on to the property. Seeing her daughter brought tears of joy to her eyes as she kissed Gina and took her to her room to help her get out of her muddy clothes. Meanwhile, she instructed Robby to squirt bubble bath into the tub and fill it with warm water.

Liz Duncan's mother always said, "When the going gets tough, the tough go to their family." This was one of those times!

After her bath, Gina joined her family for Friday-night dinner. Friday was always treated as special because it was the end of the work/school week, and the family had a full-course meal. This was especially true during basketball season. Robby needed a stick-to-your-ribs dinner before the Friday night game. Steak, mashed potatoes, and spinach were on the menu this evening. Ever since the children were very young, they were indoctrinated with the belief that spinach was the food that made muscles. Spinach omelets, spinach quiche, fresh spinach salad, spinach balls, and even spinach soup were rotated in and out of the weekly diet of the Duncan family. Mr. Duncan always told Robby to "show us your Popeyes" during the meal. This, of course, eluded to Popeye the sailor man whose strength to win over Olive Oil and defeat Brutus came from the leafy vegetable. Gina was called Sweet Pea, and his wife Olive during the playful mealtime.

Gina recounted her terrifying episode on the way home from school. When she was finished and asked if she forgave her tormentor, she said she would have to think about it. One minute later she said that yes, she forgave them, but she could not understand their cruelty.

Mr. Duncan said, "Good, let's get on with life."

Knowing Robby had to be at the gym a half hour before the game, at 7:30 p.m. he told everyone to get ready for the game.

"Do you think we should go?" questioned Mrs. Duncan. "With all that has happened, I'm not sure."

"Of course, we'll go. Do you feel up to it, my Lily Pad?"

Repeating what she had heard so many times from her father, Gina replied, "Sure thing, the Duncans are not going to let anyone or anything hold them back."

Robby added, "It's one of the biggest games of the season."

"Then let's just do it," added Mrs. Duncan.

Although the family had a good time at the game and had ice cream at Friendly's afterward, Ocean Pines came out victorious, and Robby did not have one of his better games because he was unable to concentrate on the game. The thought of the mean kids pushing his sister could not be blocked from of his mind.

19

FAT BOBBY THOMPSON, an only child, arrived home during the height of the storm. Mr. and Mrs. Thompson both worked during the day, and Bobby had been a latchkey child since he was in third grade. He would arrive home and let himself in the back door with a key that he kept on a chain around his neck. The first thing he always did was hit the refrigerator for a glass of milk, and then he would down a bag of cookies or a whole box of sugary cereal. He felt addicted to Chips Ahoy! cookies and Kellogg's Frosted Flakes. And Wise Potato Chips and Breyers Ice Cream were also consumed at an alarming rate. His parents felt they could not do anything more than they were doing to guide Bobby because they both had to work in order to pay the forever out-of-control family bills. Mrs. Stevens, the next-door neighbor, kept an eye on Bobby and the house until the parents arrived home from work. Each day, after school, she would stop in to ensure he arrived home safely. His arrival time was always a question mark because he stayed with his friends many times until late in the afternoon.

Friday at the Thompson residence was pizza night. Either Bobby's mother or father would pick up two large pepperoni pies and two large bottles of Coke on their way home from work.

Tonight Bobby only picked at his pizza. Usually he inhaled five or six pieces before he came up for a breath of air. Mr. Thompson knew there was something wrong.

"What's eating at you, big guy?" his father asked.

"Nothing, Dad, just a long day at school."

For some time, his parents had been concerned about him and not just because of his weight. Although he was very obedient, they did not approve of the friends with whom he hung around. At times they smelled cigarette smoke on his clothes. When confronted with this, Bobby claimed it was because he sometimes rode home with Victor Larson's mom, and she smoked while driving.

On a number of occasions, Mrs. Thompson told Bobby that Victor Larson and the Burris twins were bad influences and that being around them would only lead to trouble. Today she again repeated this prediction.

Out of character as he continued just nibbling on a piece of pizza, and with his face flushing redder than the pizza sauce, Bobby replied, "It already has."

Bobby relayed the happenings of the afternoon to his parents, telling them how he really didn't join in the bullying as much as the others had. His father told him that even if he just stood by without participating and did not come to the young girl's defense, he was as guilty as anyone else who participated in the pushing and name-calling.

Hanging his head in agreement, he knew his father was correct.

Mrs. Thompson nodded in affirmation as her husband continued, "Bobby, if you can't change your friends, Change Your Friends."

Not only did Bobby confess to the day's activities, he went further and told his parents about crawling in the sewer pipes and that he was smoking. He held back the fact that he also cursed when he hung out with the guys; he knew his father would be very disappointed if he knew about the bad language, and he was much too ashamed to let his mother know he used foul four-letter words.

Mrs. Thompson told him, "Honey, the first chance of moving toward forgiveness is admitting you made mistakes. The next is trying never to repeat the errors. You have done the first and easiest part. Now try to follow through by amending your ways."

From that day on, Bobby no longer associated with the Crawlers. Much like Billy Phillips, he just graduated to a better class of friends.

Not that it was easy. For over a week, after the fateful day where he started his turnaround, he continued to receive the right-palm-down greeting from the club members. At first, he pretended not to see; however, before too long, Victor and the Burris twins confronted him.

One day, after school, the three boys cornered him outside the school in the parking lot.

Victor started the assault, "Hey, fat man, you too good for us? You haven't been crawling and meeting with us under the bridge or in the Coffin."

"I know. I've been busy." He continued his lie, "My dad has been having me do chores around the house every day after school. Even on weekends he makes me wash the car, clean my room, and clean out the garage."

Larry Burris, the meaner of the twins, asked, "Does he have you vacuum the house, dust the furniture, and make all the beds too? He treats you like a little girl. A job that he should give you is cut down on all that crap you consume that keeps the rolls of dumb fat on your big, fat, dumb body."

"Come on, guys, I have just been busy."

"Ever since that incident that you refused to join in at the bridge with that Duncan kid, you have not been the same. Maybe you just got religion!" added Victor.

Just then, Coach Robinson, who was watching from his office window and knowing there was trouble brewing, walked up to the four boys.

"Get going, guys, you know there is no hanging out in the parking lot after school."

The club members walked away, leaving Bobby Thompson alone with Coach Robinson.

"I've seen a change coming over you lately and not just in gym class. Other teachers have commented about the change for the better also. It seems that you are beginning to choose your friends more wisely."

"My parents and I have had a talk about correct behavior toward others, watching with whom I hang around, and being more responsible."

"Whatever it is, it is working. You must be exercising more because it looks like you're losing weight."

Feelings of inferiority that lodged in Bobby resided deep within him; he always felt like an outcast because of his weight. He had been heavy for as long as he could remember. Victor on more than one occasion told him he had been born a big, fat, dumb blob! The encouraging words from Coach Robinson resonated within him and struck a chord of pride. He vowed to watch what he ate, cut down on snacks, and exercise by doing the chores around the house about which he lied to his former friends.

When he was in the second and third grade, teachers told Bobby that he had a gift for writing. His sentence structure and use of descriptive language was the most advanced in his class. By the time he progressed into the sixth grade, his knowledge of language arts and interest in writing classes were pushed to the side. Grades in all subjects hovered around Ds, and he failed writing and grammar, heretofore his best subject areas. In place of concern about grades came a need to be recognized and looked up to by his friends. And his peers were the rowdiest children in school.

With support of his parents and encouragement of Coach Robinson, he decided to rededicate himself to his schoolwork. His language arts teacher, Ms. Fitch, always made grammar and writing her most important teaching concern. Like being reborn, Bobby inhaled her teaching techniques, which she labeled as "The Write Stuff, Write Now." Bobby's writing skill flourished just as grass greens in the spring, and the fertilizer was the program that followed the instruction of Ms. Fitch. When it came time to write a piece on persuasion writing—that is, persuading someone to do or not do something—Bobby chose demonstrating the problems with smoking cigarettes. After the assignments were turned in to Ms. Fitch, she announced to the class that one essay was an outstanding piece of writing, and she would read it to the class. She began the class by reading Bobby Thompson's essay.

A Lifelong Habit

As people grow older, they settle into patterns of behavior developed over time that they may have a very hard time breaking. Some human activities such as the blinking of eyes and breathing are non-learned responses that come naturally; on the other hand, most good as well as actions that are not so good must be learned and reinforced so they become part of a daily routine.

Using tobacco products is one of the hardest habits to break. Because of this, it is even more difficult to quit smoking cigarettes than to teach a baby not to cry.

Pay attention to your reaction if and when these poisonous products are first introduced into the lungs.

Just as all packaging must have labels to describe the contents, packs of cigarettes contain lists of ingredients and warnings. In June 2002, based on the addictive nature of cigarette smoking, the Federal Tobacco Products Information Regulation required that "all cigarette packages display health messages that take up 50 percent of the main display surface of the package."

Everyone now knows that smoking causes cancer; the package actually gives sixteen warnings and points this out. In addition to harming the smoker, pregnant women who smoke subject their unborn child to possible problems. Additionally, secondhand smoke is harmful to nonsmokers. Later on, after smoking, smokers carry their tobacco smells with them. Be aware of the fact that breath smells. The odor of tobacco lingers on clothing and hair. Packaging also includes the fact that it is difficult to break the smoking habit. Healthline, an health watch group, claims that 85 percent of smokers are addicted to nicotine and that three-quarters try to quit with only about a 5–10 percent success rate. Add to this the fact that after smoking for a number of years, the smoker is susceptible to many physical problems. In addition to cancer, heart disease and tooth loss are common problems.

The poison, carbon monoxide, is contained in cigarette smoke. Millions of older people now have COPD (chronic obstruction pulmonary disease) and cigarette smoking is the leading cause! Beginning of smoking is many times attributed to thinking you need to smoke to belong. The experience of the desire to rebel that is common during adolescence may also lead to smoking. When someone is raised in a home with smokers, there is a greater tendency to pick up this habit. Parental smoking is many times passed down to children.

And if older siblings smoke, don't you think there is a good chance that the younger brothers and sisters will too?

Never start the nasty habit of smoking because of peer pressure and outside influences around you. If you do smoke, then take steps necessary to quit. Nicotine gum and patches are available to help kick the habit. New medications are constantly arriving on the market to help win the battle over addiction. Some success has even been demonstrated by acupuncture.

The learned behavior of smoking cigarettes may be unlearned; however, it is a very difficult victory to achieve.

If you have ever tried smoking, listen to your body's first reaction of coughing and dizziness. Better yet, don't ever try it in the first place.

When Ms. Fitch was done reading, the class applauded wildly, as if the basketball team had just won the county championship. Bobby was beet red, so everyone knew it was his work that had been read. Now, you could be sure that no Crawler would every associate with anyone who actually tried in school and had been singled out for academic work! By the time Bobby graduated from the seventh grade, he also graduated to a new class of friends.

20

ROBBY'S TEMPERATURE CONTINUED to spike. At times it would seem to be under control as it came down from 103.5 to 100 degrees. On day three in the ICU, things seemed to be improving; although Gina was not allowed to visit her brother, her parents tried to explain to her what was happening.

Mrs. Duncan said, "The body contains bacteria. Some of it is good and necessary, but sometimes bad bacteria or germs get into us, and they settle in different parts of the body, causing an infection. For Robby, bad bacteria have gotten into his bloodstream, and must be killed with medicine."

"Pumpkin Roll, those little buggers are sometimes hard to conquer. This is why it takes time to win the battle," added Mr. Duncan. "It is kind of like a 'Who done it,' as they figure out who the bad guys are, and then they decide how to best take care of them."

In Gina's mind, she thought of the mystery of Robby's germ problem like the game of Clue. In time the killer would be isolated to a specific room and weapon, and the crime would be solved ("*Mr. Green did it in the library with the revolver*"). After this, Robby would be back home with her, and Nanny would be running around in the yard playing with them. Things would soon return to normal!

The infection doctor, Dr. Fischer, stopped by in the early afternoon each day as he made his rounds in the hospital. Not satisfied with progress, two new powerful antibiotics were added to combat

Robby's fluctuating temperature. Imipenem and Zosyn were introduced, and these finally brought the infection under control. Robby was allowed to go home on a Tuesday. He had to keep the line from his right arm in place and going to heart; a nurse met the family at home and showed Mrs. Duncan how to give Robby his intravenous medication. The process and order of giving drugs went by the acronym SASH. First clean the injection site on the line going to the heart with saline, followed by antibiotic, then saline again, and finally heparin.

Robby began his summer vacation from Deergrove School three weeks after graduation when he was finally released from the hospital. This was two weeks after his operation to separate his joined fingers. Staying in the house, his mother gave him his medicine through the PIC line three times a day and took his temperature twice a day, in the morning and in the afternoon. While Robby was away at the hospital, Nanny moped around the house as if she lost her best friend, which, in reality, she had. Not knowing how to act in Robby's absence, this usually quiet and calm animal bit her front paws until they were raw. During sleep, she would put her paws over her eyes and moan and yip quietly as if she were dreaming about days gone by when she played with Robby. While in the yard, she chased her tail as she circled around and around, trying to comfort herself. After Robby returned home, Nanny's nervous behavior ceased, and she again settled into her content conduct of nestling herself against him as he sat in a chair or reclined on the coach to receive his daily dosages of medication.

All was going well until six days later when his temperature again began to rise. The first to sense the change, Nanny paced back and forth in front of Robby; she caught a whiff, and what she smelled made her unable to lie down. After sliding back and forth for a few minutes as if she were doing a country line dance, she stood at attention at her master's side. Like a bodyguard ready to pounce on an unforeseen assailant, she froze, staring straight ahead before resuming her dance in front of him.

It was Monday evening when Mrs. Duncan called Dr. Gottlieb to make him aware that Robby again had a temperature over 103 degrees. After getting the answering service and being connected to the doctor on duty, she was asked if he could hold out from seeing a doctor until three days later, Thursday, when he was scheduled for a follow-up visit with Dr. Gottlieb. Tuesday morning Robby was no better, and he was delirious with fever. Dr. Gottlieb had clinic hours at his office at South Shore County Hospital on Tuesdays, so Mrs. Duncan called and was told to bring Robby in to see the doctor.

When they arrived, Dr. Gottlieb told them that the line going to his heart was infected and that it would have to be taken out. The catheter was slowly pulled from its resting place at the entry to the right atrium and out of the vein. Then a new line was inserted into Robby's left arm so he could continue to receive the strong antibiotics into his bloodstream as the blood completed its circuit and reentered his pumping organ.

Robby was admitted again to the ICU where he could have his temperature monitored twenty-four hours a day. Checking the heart showed that although the vegetation was not as obvious as it had been previously, small waves of plantlike life continued to sway with the opening and closing of his valves.

Once his temperature returned to below 99 degrees, Robby was taken to the heart station to have his heart examined. Because no abnormalities could be detected, he was allowed to return home and continue taking his medication through the PIC line. A follow-up with his heart doctor was scheduled for the following week.

After seemingly an endless week at home, Dr. Fischer let Mrs. Duncan know that the battle with infection in his heart was now finally being won, and the line that fed him medication would soon be taken from his left arm. It was determined that the mitral valve was squeezing only about 65 percent of the blood through the heart, and further examination of the continuing arrhythmia, heart-pumping problem, would be necessary. A more-invasive electrophysiological study, a catherization, was scheduled for the next day.

Mrs. Duncan asked Dr. Fisher, "How long will the procedure take, and how dangerous is it?"

"It is done in the cauterization lab and takes a couple hours from start to finish." He continued, "Robby will be put under general anesthetic, and small electrodes will be inserted up to his heart through his groin. After that, the electrodes will be fired to mimic the electrical stimulus generated by the heart at about eighty times per minute. It is a wonderful tool to check the flow of the pulsing pathways through the heart, which is much like the flow of electricity through the power lines that come into our homes. It is very safe, and I will be there throughout the examination."

It was further explained that if an abnormality in the firing of the pulses through the heart were found, an operation to insert a device to keep the electrical heart impulses in balance would be necessary to restore correct synchronization between the heart rate and the pulse.

Robby's test showed no problems with the electrical system of his heart, and he was sent home to continue his battle with the bacterial invaders. With Nanny again able to relax at his side, he continued his uphill climb on the slippery slope of recovery. By the end of the summer, he was sufficiently recovered and free of infection. Antibiotics were discontinued, and he was ready to begin his four years at Deergrove High School.

21

DETERMINED TO PUT her past insecurities behind her, Gina entered the eighth grade. It seemed that she was becoming invisible less and less often as her past fears were being addressed and conquered. Ongoing weekly counseling sessions in which she participated since third grade were now held only monthly, and she felt she was graduating to a life of greater confidence when dealing with others both in and away from school. She was coming to realize that fears, like hatred, are like heavy building blocks that got so unmanageable over time they could not personally be carried any longer. Being afraid all the time and giving in to irrational fears only led to panic spiraling out of control. Gina learned that addressing her emotional concerns and reasons behind them was a much better way to handle problems than withdrawing within herself and retreating into a hidden world. Even without her brother at school—Robby was now at high school and unable to give her daily support at school—Gina grew both mentally and physically into a new more confident young lady.

With a chance for a new life of normalcy, Gina thought of the beginning of her eighth-grade school year as the time of her rebirth. Now she told herself she would "go with the flow" and no longer run and become invisible when she felt uncomfortable. Imagined demons stopped invading her sleep, and for the first time in as long as she could remember, she began to wake up each morning feeling rested and looking forward to beginning a new day.

Ms. Tina Grant from dancing school had a daughter, Mary Beth, who was in Gina's class at school. Of course, they were in dancing classes together too. Mary Beth Grant valued her friendship with Gina that flourished throughout seventh grade; they became inseparable as they entered eighth grade. Joining together with the friendship of Samantha Phillips, the three girls seemed to always be together. Mrs. Duncan, who had a few very close friends, knew how important it was for girls to have friends. She was determined that Gina would not continue to grow up in isolation, without peers to share hopes, dreams, and fantasy for the future. She took the three friends wherever they wanted to go: to the movies, shopping at the mall, visiting amusement parks, and many other places. Mrs. Duncan would stay in the background and allow the girls to have their private conversations on many topics which she knew included boys; like a mother hen, she simply looked after the girls during their excursions and did not impose her adultness on them.

Mr. Duncan referred to the Gina and her friends as The Three Minkees. A fan of Peter Sellers and the *Pink Panther* movies, he would often ask Gina what was new with the Minkees, and Gina did not mind as long as he only called them that when they were not present.

Mrs. Duncan was a theme person. Each room was outfitted with a distinct personality. The kitchen's topic, where the family usually had their meals, was apples; the place looked like an apples-gone-wild! The curtains had apples on them. There was an apple clock that kept track of apple time. Apple-shaped salt-and-pepper shakers sat on the tablecloth which blossomed with apples. The napkin holder and napkins were decorated with apples, the centerpiece on the table was an apple-embossed bowl filled with apples, and apple stencils encircled the top of the walls. There were red apples, there were green apples, and there were yellow apples everywhere! Mr. Duncan not so secretly told his children that their mother was an "apple-holic."

"What's new with the Minkees? What have you guys been up to, Tadpole?" he asked one Friday evening during dinner in the orchard.

"Not much, Dad. Tomorrow we are trying out for the cheer-leading squad."

Robby chimed in, "All three of you can't miss. When I was play-ing for the basketball team, the cheerleaders really tried, but they were a bit awkward. They did not have the abilities you guys have. You can dance and move together. I'll have to come to football games to see you in action. I'm trying out for the freshman basketball team, so I don't know if I'll be able to see you doing your thing during all those games if I make the team."

"We haven't even had one tryout yet!"

Mrs. Duncan added, "Cheerleaders have never come from Ms. Tina's Dancing School. I don't know that the school is ready for really talented cheerleaders. Gina, how many children will be going out for the team, and how many will make it?"

"I don't know, Mom. Last year there were twelve girls cheering, and I was told that more than twenty were hopeful of being chosen."

Mr. Duncan bellowed, "Cuddle Bunny, we can practice right after we are finished eating. Get on the horn and call the Minkees."

The next morning seventh and eighth-grade hopefuls showed up in the gym at Deergrove School. To no one's surprise, all three dancers made the grade. The newfound notoriety of becoming a cheerleader helped Gina greatly as she continued her personal ado-lescent development. Her character was beginning to take shape like clay in the hands of a master potter, and she no longer viewed herself as a stranger in a strange land.

22

MR. AND MRS. Thompson began to notice a change in their son, Bobby. Like watching grains of sand descend in an hourglass, transformation was slow and gradual yet perceptible. As he started the seventh grade, he no longer hung out after school, and the smell of cigarette smoke attributed to Mrs. Phillips no longer lingered in his hair and on his clothes.

An interest in girls in school, especially Gina Duncan, caused him to take better care of his general appearance. He stopped filling his free time by gobbling down snacks, and he began working out with the weights his parents bought for him two years earlier for his tenth birthday. He actually portioned his meals, abandoning his prior need to shovel huge amounts of sugar and starch into his now-shrinking belly. And he broke an unwritten rule of his former Crawler companions; he began playing sports at Deergrove School. Because of his size, he played football. As a seventh grader, he started off at right offensive guard on the eighth-grade team. He transitioned to middle linebacker the following year. As the pounds came off and he demonstrated newfound speed and agility, Bobby became the star of the defense. He hoped to continue his success in high school the next year at Deergrove High School.

During football games, Bobby was always the first one to arrive and get dressed. He always sat on a bench in the same exact spot in the locker room, dressed and ready for action well before other players arrived and the whistle to start the game sounded. He took pride in his slimmed-down appearance, and his need to be punctual in all things he did was like a chronic yet very under-control, manageable illness. Time that seemed to tick inside him without skipping a second saw him on time for school, football practice, exercising with his weights, being home after school, and having meals with his family. Happiness bathed him, cleansing him of past excesses, as Bobby contently completed his weekly routine.

Sports and superstition seemed to go hand in hand. In addition to having to be the first player dressed before games, Bobby always put his playing equipment on in a set order. Wearing his lucky T-shirt, he first put his shoulder pads on. Following this, he slipped into football jersey, pants first and shirt second. But before he put his uniform on, he had to put on his left sock and left football shoe. With his uniform in place, secured by his father's belt, he then put on his right sock and right football cleat. Then he laced his shoes with a double bow, always tying the left one before the right. He believed that if the order of getting his gear in place were not followed exactly, he would have a bad game. Worse, the team would definitely lose!

During Deergrove School's season with eighth-grader Bobby leading the way on to the field, the cheerleaders would begin chanting, "Let's go, Knights. Let's go, Knights." As contests at both home and away games were played, everyone knew that although the football team might not lead the conference in victories, the girls that supported them were the most talented on Long Island. Gina, Amy, and Mary Beth were the tri-captains of this exceptional squad of young ladies. Using their sense of rhythm, accompanied with dancing moves never seen before on the sidelines, the usual chant of, "Defense, Defense," took on new meaning. And no one could be happier with their support than Bobby, who flew around the playing field with reckless abandon, knocking down would-be blockers and smothering the ball carrier.

The Duncan family, to include Robby, was in attendance at most of the home football games to show support for the team as well as for the cheerleaders. Tina Grant volunteered to help coach the girls and teach them synchronized moves and flips as well as develop innovative cheers. She held free classes twice a week at her dancing school to teach the girls new routines. "We are Knights and are days A-bove the rest, A-bove the rest, -A-bove the rest, A-bove the rest. We are the Best," boasted backflips by half the squad as "A-bove" was chanted into the megaphones and echoed back by the team supporters in the stands. Channel 12 petitioned the school, and the girls had their cheers videotaped. This public television station showed the cheerleaders in a segment aired on two consecutive Saturday mornings. This notoriety brought recognition to Deergrove School as well as caused poise and confidence to soar in Gina and her fellow cheerleaders.

The succession in the ranks of the Crawlers, much like many formal and informal organizations, always seemed to pass from an older brother on down to a younger sibling. When Victor Larson, who might well have been the meanest leader ever to guide the group, felt he was too old and too cool to crawl, his younger brother, Sammy, took over the leadership role. Although not as sinister as his brother, if an award for name-calling could be given, Sammy would win first prize! In seventh grade and younger than Gina by a year, he rode the yellow bus with her to school and began the year calling her names; however, by this time, Gina's sense of self had undergone a remarkable transformation and was well developed. When she was called Frog Feet and asked, "Are you going out for the swim team with your flipper feet?" she simply reacted with a pleasant smile. Other attempts to put down Gina by Sammy were always handled by her in the same manner. Like all bullies and big mouths, when the person you were trying to make feel inferior did not cooperate by crying, sulking, or shrinking away, frustration with the would-be target sank in, so they moved on to another victim. In the case of Sammy, the older eighth-grade children told him to shut up and go crawl in a hole. And there were no obvious victims waiting to be brutalized. The popularity of the Crawlers as well as the membership was withering away like a houseplant dying from lack of sun and water. The younger boys in Deergrove were content to stay indoors, playing computer games and the new craze, surfing the internet. Crawlers were becoming a dying breed.

23

ROBBY CONTINUED PLAYING basketball at Deergrove High School, and he was the captain and starred on the freshman team. During his second year, as his talents on the court continued to develop, he was easily the best player on the junior varsity team. The varsity team started off the year losing their first three games; consequently, Robby was moved up to this team. With much older players, at six feet three inches tall, he was moved into a starting forward position. Able to handle the ball, shoot with tremendous outside range, and soar above opposing players as he drove to the hoop, he was an imposing player who would dunk during games over players four and five inches taller than he was. Although it took him a few weeks to adjust to performing with bigger and more mature athletes, by the end of the year, he was a pivotal member of the squad that finished with a respectable eight-win, seven-loss season.

As Robby's body continued to grow and develop, his hands did also. Two years after the operation, his problem was not too noticeable; nevertheless, the two fingers that were separated had a perceptible difference in color from the rest of his hand. Since the grafted skin came from a different part of his body, it did not react to sunlight in the same manner as the tissue covering the other fingers. And where the middle and ring finger had been joined, growth at the point where they separated from the hand showed webbing because of his inherited deformity. During his second year of college, Dr. Gottlieb performed a second operation that everyone knew would be necessary. In comparison to the first procedure, this was a rather simple process, and it was completed without any of the complications that were experienced six and a half years earlier. The previous cojoined fingers still did not function as well as his other eight digits because of bone separation that was necessary during the first surgical procedure. The joints were inflexible above the bottom knuckle; accordingly, it was difficult to make a fist. Except for not being able to pursue a career as a boxer or entering a cage as a mixed martial combatant, Robby knew he would be able to lead a normal life! His problem would never hold him back from accomplishing anything he desired to do.

Gina, now a freshman at Deergrove High, helped support her brother and the football team by cheering during games. Overcoming her social fears and accepting the fact that there would always be losers who delighted in making others feel badly, she became more popular and outgoing. Throughout her high school years, Gina continued on her path of self-dependence and self-respect. Leaving the retreat of her isolated nest, she spread her wings and was recognized as a leader by the other students. By the time she graduated, her classmates would vote her as "The Most Likely to Succeed," as she continued to adjust to high school children around her. As president of the student council, she became involved in school politics; the interpersonal skills she developed helped guide her toward her career choice as a school counselor for middle-school children.

Bobby Thompson continued to play football; however, he blew out a knee during his junior year in high school and was no longer able to play this grueling sport. He kept control of his weight by exercising daily and by watching what he ate. He was editor-in-chief of his high school paper, *The Knighthood*. Years later he joined the police force; he was assigned to the precinct run by Captain Thomas Duncan, his future father-in-law, who years before had such a profound influence on his life. And he continued to write. He authored *The Policeman's Code of Conduct* that was instituted throughout all the precincts of Nassau and Suffolk Counties. And he didn't stop there. Becoming a noted author, his specialty genre was mystery novels, and he called upon his many experiences in the crime investigation to weave interesting plots into his stories.

As a master electrician, Victor Larson worked in various communities throughout Long Island. As sprawling developments continued to pop up in both Nassau and Suffolk counties, he never lacked work. Vowing to not repeat the actions of his father by running away from familial responsibility, he became a dedicated husband and father. His brother, Sammy, did not make out quite so well. He continued to fall in with a bad crowd and was arrested for possession of marijuana with intent to sell. The rocky road of drug addiction saw him involved in crime to help support his habit. He did not learn his lesson until after he was arrested for holding up a 7-Eleven store. After serving two years in Nassau County Prison, he took advantage of another chance at life and became a respectable member of the community.

The Burris twins became bodybuilders. All their free time was spent supporting each other at the gym. They lifted weights together; Louis watched what Larry ate, and Larry watched what Louis ate. They ran through the streets of Deergrove together. Working side by side at the local distribution center for Sears, they were able to lift and carry twice as much weight as any other warehouse employees. They became sports enthusiasts. Traveling to Madison Square Garden in Manhattan, they never missed a Ranger ice hockey home game. Holding season tickets for the New York Yankees, they sported Yankee hats wherever they went. The brothers attended professional championship wrestling matches at the Nassau Coliseum; and when Wrestlemania came to town, they decided on a career change, entering the ring as "The Flying Burrises From Parts Unknown." Heavily tattooed, the tag team strutted around the ring like peacocks, flexing their muscles and showing off their body art. Their abilities to berate and put down others served them well in this sport that relied so heavily on bad-mouthing your opponents.

Once the Crawlers disbanded, never to resurface again, the youth of Deergrove took refuge in their homes to play video games and watch big-screen television. Most of them tried in school and took on part-time jobs in the community. They became meaningful members of society, raising families and living in the various towns in Nassau and Suffolk counties, adding to the prosperity of Long Island.

About the Author

ONE OF SEVEN children, Richard Betz grew up in a competitive yet tumultuous family in a densely populated town on Long Island, New York. After graduating from Loyola University in Baltimore, he spent a year playing professional basketball in Europe and then went on to earn a master's degree from Fordham University. After spending more than twenty years in the corporate sector, he spent ten years as a middle school teacher. For the fictional town of Deergrove, he draws from his experiences of seeing the cruelty and forgiveness of others.

During his years teaching as well as in his formative years, Richard witnessed positive as well as negative leadership qualities as children struggled to adapt, fit in, and belong. The problem of bullying is evident, and the necessity for childhood adjustment is woven throughout the lives of young adults.

Richard currently resides in Florida and enjoys golfing, writing, and travel with his wife.

CPSIA information can be obtained
at www.ICGtesting.com
Printed in the USA
BVHW070743080921
616221BV00001B/218